Nasir

AN EMOTIONAL SCARS, BODYGUARD, ROMANTIC
SUSPENSE

TN SEAL SECURITY BOOK
BOOK TWO

CHIQUITA DENNIE

304 PUBLISHING COMPANY

Copyright © 2022 by Chiquita Dennie

For questions and comments about this book, please contact 304 Publishing at 304publishing@gmail.com. Visit the official website at www.chiquitadennie.com

❀ Created with Vellum

Latest Releases

Latest Releases from Chiquita Dennie

The Early Years-A Prequel Short Story

Until Serena (HEA World Novel)
Antonio and Sabrina: Struck in Love 5
Heart of Stone, Book 4 (Jessica and Joseph)
She's All I Need
Red Light District (A Fantasy Romance Short)
Summer Break Book 1
The Carrington Cartel Book 1
Betrayed: Fuertes Mafia Cartel Book 3
Something Gained (A Romantic Comedy Book1)
Upcoming Releases (2023/2024):
The Carrington Cartel Book 2
Fall For You (Satin Hill Book1)
Dare To Love
Unveiled (Achille Cartel Book 1)

Disclaimer

This work of fiction contains strong language, violence, and explicit sexual content and is only intended for mature readers. This story may contain uncomfortable situations, language, and sexual encounter that may offend some readers. This book is for mature readers 18+.

Introduction

Grab some wine and get ready for more spicy, sinful, sexy suspense.

Are you signed up for my newsletter?

Join today and find out all the latest in new releases, contests, giveaways, sneak peeks, and more.

www.chiquitadennie.com

Synopsis

Cyrah is used to the limelight; people fall at her feet to be next to her at events. When she becomes entangled in a major public incident because of her ex, she stumbles onto a bigger conspiracy with deadly intentions.

Navy Seal Nasir has dealt with his share of high-profile clients, but when he protects a high-value target from a sniper's bullet, he finds himself in the middle of an Assassin terror plot.

Now he feels compelled to keep Cyrah safe. The only question is, will the fiercely independent and outspoken actress accept his help?

CHAPTER 1
Nasir

THE RIDE in the van was quiet as we headed to the Chicago Toyota Center for the second game of the basketball finals. Nicco was driving, and two guys were in the back, along with two more vans following. Tonight's mission was to protect the governor and his guest, the visiting president of France.

Aydin was out on a date with his wife, so tonight, I was the lead on this assignment, and we'd gone over every scenario. The game started in twenty minutes, and according to the last update I'd received, people were still lining up.

We checked our equipment and pulled on our vests. Then we scheduled a meeting with the governor at the back door. Ten minutes later, Nicco arrived and turned at the light as I scanned the crowd of people passing through the checkpoint. He pulled into the back entrance, where the teams had arrived and parked.

"How much did you bet tonight?" Nicco turned the van off and popped the door open.

"Shit. Probably a grand on my team winning," I joked,

knowing the Chicago Tigers were the top team in the league, and the Los Angeles Hawks didn't stand a chance.

We'd sweep in four.

"Aydin's going to kick your ass when he finds out," Nicco taunted and shut the door behind him.

I climbed out, and the rest of the team lined up, double-checking their earpieces.

Honk!

A black stretch limo pulled in behind us, and the governor stepped out with French President Antonie Bernard. Nicco and I approached and shook hands with their security.

"Governor, we have you ready," I responded with a shake of my hand.

"President Bernard, this is Nasir of the TN Seal Security. I've worked with them for other events," Governor Johns said, clapping me on the shoulder.

"Nice to meet you, Nasir. I hope you don't mind. I brought a few of my security personnel with me." President Bernard spoke with a French accent.

"No problem, as long as they know we're in charge. They'll be posted out front," I explained, pulling up the schematics of the area on my phone.

"I trust them and will have a good time tonight," Governor Johns announced and motioned for Nicco to show where they'd be for the night.

"You can follow me because the game's about to start." I lifted my wrist to check the time. Kickoff was about to happen, and I knew they probably wanted drinks and food.

At first, I'd wanted them in the VIP suites upstairs. However, the governor had insisted on sitting with the regular spectators, so they'd reserved seats on the fourth row in the bleachers. I focused in front of me and checked in with my men over the earpiece.

"You'll love the playoff game. The best team in the world." Governor Johns boasted about Chicago as the usher motioned them to their seats.

I followed and looked again underneath each seat. People started to pile in and fill the section. We had eight seats behind and in front as a precaution.

"Ladies and gentlemen, welcome to game two of the basketball playoffs," the announcer called, and tip-off started.

I removed the binoculars and scanned the crowd. Nothing stood out as the game began.

"Come on, Chicago!" Governor Johns shouted, getting excited.

"How are things out front?" I asked on the walkie-talkie.

"On my end, good," Nicco replied, staring at the scene with eyes on the fans.

"Good," the rest of the team answered.

I angled upward to the big screen and watched them put the camera on the governor and French president. Most of the people clapped and stood up. Some booed, but that came with the territory of politics.

A few people did the wave when the home team scored, and I smirked, knowing Nicco would owe me a grand after tonight.

Pop!

"Argghhh!"

The noise settled down, and I looked again at the crowd, then VIP suites. I could have sworn I saw a figure move. I shook it out of my mind. I glanced at the governor, then the president, seeing him slip and fall.

"Mr. President!" I barked and moved quickly to check his pulse.

"What's going on?" Governor Johns yelled. The noise drowned him out.

"Governor, we need to move. Now!" I lifted President

Bernard on my shoulder, and security helped to shield him as people started to look in our direction at the commotion.

"Nicco! Eagle down. Get your car ready," I demanded into the walkie-talkie.

"On the way," Nicco replied as we rushed through the crowd, shoving people out of the way.

"What happened?" French detail called out, removing him from my grasp.

"It was too fast; all I saw was him slumped over. He has a pulse."

They gathered him in the ambulance, and the governor climbed into the limo. Nicco ran up to us.

"The VIP suites were supposed to be closed for the night, correct?" I stared at each of the men, including Nicco. He was the second in command and knew I liked things to be triple-checked. Nothing like this should happen on my watch.

"Someone had to make a call last-minute if one was open," Jasper, one of my men, blurted.

I agreed. "Get the general manager now, and let's leave. I want everything locked down. However, I need to keep the game going."

Canceling the game and having people storming out would make things worse. I needed to keep them occupied long enough to look at camera footage and check the place out one more time. Whoever had done this was a professional, maybe in the military.

Nicco talked on the phone as I waved for the housekeeper to unlock the door.

"You two go check the next room. Nothing to be thrown away until you lay your eyes on it, am I clear?" I commanded.

Jasper and Chris nodded and headed to the next suite on the floor.

I told the housekeeper to stay out while Nicco and I

checked the place out. The room looked spotless. Nicco entered the bathroom, and I checked the seats out and went to the window.

"Clear in here," Nicco yelled.

I pushed the window sideways without touching it and angled my binoculars down to the section where the governor had been sitting. It was a perfect shot. I turned to see Jasper in the next suite.

"Nothing here!" Jasper shouted, bewilderment in his voice.

"I want fingerprints done. We probably won't get anything, but we need to be sure."

Ring!

"Aydin." I unlocked my phone to answer the call and walked out of the room to let in forensics.

"All over the news," Aydin said in disappointment.

"Who talked?" I turned an accusatory stare toward the people around me.

"Probably a few fans, but you need to get up to the hospital."

I frowned. "Is he going to be all right?"

"He's in surgery. Not sure."

"Shit!" I ran a hand across my face.

"Don't blame yourself," Aydin replied.

"Yeah, I hear you." I ended the call, gripping the phone in my hand. Heading toward the van, I opened the passenger door.

"You ready?" Nicco climbed in.

I looked at each police officer as they conducted interviews with the arena staff as we drove out of the building.

———

"I'm calling a meeting in the morning." I flipped through the videos and social media of what had happened.

Nicco sped into the front entrance of the hospital's emergency room and parked. He pushed the door open. "Already told the guys, sleep won't happen for a while."

I shut the door behind me and stalked into the hospital. I showed my badge to security, and they allowed my team inside.

"Make sure we have every employee's name, and everyone is searched before they leave," I informed Nicco, patting his chest and stalking into the waiting room up to the nursing station.

"Nasir!"

I turned at the governor's voice and met him at the employee door.

"How is he?"

As he rubbed the back of his neck, the governor led me through the doors into his room. Outside, security stood watch.

"Still in surgery. They gave me a room after checking me over," Governor Johns explained.

Since the person who'd pulled the trigger was still on the loose, I didn't want him to be out in the open for too long.

"We need to get you back home." My heart felt like a fist pounding the inside of my chest.

The governor waved me off, folding his hands in front of him. "Nasir, I'm not leaving until I know he's safe."

All eyes shifted straight to him. The door across the hall opened, and I heard loud yelling.

"Ma'am, she can't leave right now," the nurse was saying to a woman.

"I don't pay you to think," a smooth, velvety voice replied.

"Cyrah, hush." The older woman with the nurse pointed into the room.

The governor's doctor came over, and I shifted my attention back to them.

"Doctor Fox, is he going to be all right?" Governor Johns questioned.

"It was touch and go for a moment, but he's in recovery," Doctor Fox answered.

"Great. Can we see him?" I asked.

"Get the doctor over here. This is ridiculous!"

My gaze was drawn to the woman again. She had a bandage across her forehead. Something about her was familiar, but I couldn't figure out where I knew her from. I could clearly see her beauty across the hallway. The light fell on her warm, golden skin, her full lips, and high cheekbones.

"What are you looking at?" she spat.

I cleared my throat and turned my focus back to the doctor.

"He's with another patient. Please go back to bed." The nurse tried to escort her back to the room, but the woman snatched her arm away.

"Do you know who I am? I don't have time to wait!" she snapped.

I glared at her as I marched toward them.

"Hey!" The older woman stepped in front of me, her lips creased into a thin line. "You're not supposed to be back here! I'll call the police," she shouted, poking me in the chest.

"What?" I asked, confused.

"Call the police. Photographers aren't supposed to be back here," the younger woman said.

"I'm not a photographer." Warning bells went off in my head.

She raised her hand to cut me off. "I don't take pictures, and you're violating my privacy," she continued, her words clipped.

"First off, your loud ass is interrupting this entire floor of sick people."

"Excuse me?" A gasp escaped her lips.

"You're excused, but the nurse is trying to help, and you're giving her a hard time." I pointed at the nurse next to me, who smiled gratefully.

"Are you supposed to be back here?" the older woman asked.

"Listen, we can't have this going on. Cyrah, I'll have the doctor talk with you as soon as he's finished," the nurse directed.

"Should have done that twenty minutes ago." Cyrah turned and went back to her room.

"Try and keep your voices down," I pressed, and she flipped me off.

"My daughter doesn't take orders from you," her mom concluded.

"There will be trouble if your daughter draws more attention to this hallway." I glanced over her head to her daughter in bed, and she pushed the curtain around to block my view.

———

After closing the door of my black Jeep Cherokee, I lifted the coffee to my lips. I balanced the other coffee in my hand and inserted my security code into the front door. Molly waved at me, and I carried the second cup to her.

"You are the best, Nasir." Molly gripped both sides of the cup, closed her eyes, and took a sip.

"I know. Any updates from Nicco?"

Molly nodded her head and picked up the stack of messages.

I glanced over to the computer screen and saw a

familiar face. "What are you watching?" Darkness crossed my face.

Molly looked over at her computer. "My favorite movie, *Rush into Love* with Cyrah Brinkley," Molly answered, sitting in the chair.

"I know her." I pointed at the computer.

"Who?" She turned to me, her face lighting up as she spoke.

"Her." I walked over to the screen and tapped on the woman she'd indicated.

"Wait, you know Cyrah Brinkley? How, where?" Molly put her cup down on the desk and focused on me.

"Last night at the hospital."

"The hospital." She mulled over my words.

"Yeah, last night with the shooting, I had to check on the governor and president of France."

"How are they?"

"He's in a private room now under surveillance."

"So where does Cyrah Brinkley come into all of this?"

"Cyrah Brinkley?" Amelia approached her desk.

"Nasir met her last night," Molly explained.

"Really? I haven't talked to her in a while. She was out of town filming," Amelia informed us.

Molly's eyes bucked wide. "You know Cyrah Brinkley?"

"A family friend." Amelia gave a little wisp of a smile.

"Whoever she is, the woman is atrocious," I recalled, heading down the hall and leaving them to talk.

I unlocked my door, dropped my bag on the ground, stretched, and placed my coffee on the desk. We'd worked with celebrities before, and all of them had been approachable and respectful in person, but this Cyrah person took it to another level.

Knock! Knock!

I lifted my eyes and saw Nicco at the door. He seemed

to not be in the best mood like me. Anytime a mission went wrong, it hit us hard. My mind raced with every movement we'd made from the original timeline of us in the car coming to the venue.

As he approached the chair, I gestured for him to sit down. "What's the update? Preliminary file ready?"

"About that." Nicco plopped down in the chair and passed the folder to me.

I sat on the edge of the desk and opened it to the briefing of the night everything had gone down. Alarms went off in my head of where I went wrong.

"After you left, it was hard to get the reports on the French president."

"Why?" I looked up at him, flipping to the next page.

"Because Cyrah Brinkley was on the same floor, and they locked it down." Nicco sounded pissed as he leaned forward and clasped his hands in his lap.

I frowned. "Locked it down?"

"Yeah. Her manager or lawyer barred the photographers. They had the hospital kick everyone off the floor except immediate family."

"That bitch." It came out in a stern tone as I scanned the notes of interviews from the governor and his team.

"He's supposed to be discharged in a few days." A grimace wrinkled his face.

"I'm not waiting that long." With each revelation, my antenna told me something was off about this case.

"What about we go talk to the police and his team first?"

"You should talk to his team, and I'll speak to the police."

"Meeting!" Jasper came to the door and yelled.

"I'm sure Aydin will have something to say about everything," Nicco remarked as I walked to the conference room where we reviewed missions.

Nicco held the door open, and Amelia came in first,

with us following behind. Aydin smiled and winked at her as he often did since they got married.

The meeting started with Amelia sitting next to me and Aydin talking through each of the jobs for the month. My attention was drawn to the folder in front of me as I replayed the shooting timeline. I noticed Amelia's phone vibrated with an interesting name.

Buzz!

Amelia reached for the phone as *Cyrah* called again, but she didn't answer.

CHAPTER 2
Cyrah

"HOLD YOUR HEAD UP," Tanja said. She was our makeup artist for today's filming.

I put the water bottle down on the counter. Sitting back in my chair, I crossed my legs and attempted to be still while she put me together. Last night replayed in my mind at the hospital after I'd passed out on set. My mother and I had to fight tooth and nail to keep the new of me in the hospital away from prying photographers.

I'd finally gotten to a point in my career as a top actress where I could pick and choose my roles. My personal life was a different story because I challenged how things were presented to the world when a false story was reported. Most times, when I called out bullshit, I got a text from my publicist and agent to delete my social media and let the press speculate, but I wasn't the type of person to let people lie about me.

"Are you ready for today's shoot?" Tanja asked. "It's a long day today."

"For the most part. I took a few Advil, so hopefully, they'll clear my head."

"What did they say? What caused you to faint?"

Tanja was cool but shady. She loved to get the latest gossip, then sell it to the highest bidder. I'd kept her around for so long because she did great work.

"Just needed some rest." I leaned forward in the mirror to check my makeup.

Tanja stood behind me. "You work too much."

"I know. My time is limited between filming and trying to produce outside projects."

"Time for a vacation." Tanja picked up the brush and pulled the rollers out of my hair one by one.

"My mom won't let that happen."

"Mommy dearest," Tanja kidded.

As if on cue, the trailer door opened and my mother came stepped in. "How much longer, Tanja?" she inquired.

Tanja brushed my hair out, and I lifted the water bottle to my lips to avoid another talk.

"Probably twenty minutes, Miss Sable," Tanja replied.

"Make that five minutes. You've slacked off for the past few weeks."

Tanja's eyes ballooned wide in exasperation at my mom's controlling ways.

"Sable, can you be reasonable, please and give her fifteen minutes?" I suggested.

She narrowed her eyes at me for speaking back in front of Tanja. "We have to make up for your lack of presence, or did you forget?"

"Sorry I got sick, but it's out of my control."

"You going out and partying is the problem, or did you forget what I've done for you?"

I waited for her to go into her same story about putting her life on hold to help support my dream of being an actress.

"Mom."

"Call me Sable, and Tanja, you have five minutes," Mom

instructed, tapping her watch before turning and leaving the trailer.

"Can you grab my coffee? Oh, and don't forget to pick up my dry cleaning." I ran off my to-do list for my mom.

"You have five minutes, Cyrah!" Sable yelled.

"Hold still, Cyrah," Tanja fussed as I reached to grab my phone.

I rolled my eyes and continued to scroll through my log of notes. I had a full day on set for filming, then I could relax for the rest of the week.

Ring!

"I have to take this call." I held my hand up for Tanja to pause, slid out of the chair, and stood off to the side.

"Cyrah?"

"Amelia! It's been forever since we've talked."

"I know. I'm sorry to get back to you so late." Amelia sounded aggravated.

"Amelia, do you want this drink or not?" I heard a deep voice in the background.

"Nasir, I'm on the phone." I heard ruffling like someone was fighting.

"Who is this?" a deep, raspy voice questioned.

I pulled the phone from my ear. "Excuse me?"

"You're excused, sweetheart, but I need you to call her back." His smugness came through the phone.

"My name is not *sweetheart*, jackass!"

I heard chuckling, then a dial tone. I pulled my phone away from my ear in disbelief. He'd hung up on me. My eyes rolled skyward, and I blew out a breath. "What the hell was that?" I murmured and dialed Amelia back.

"Hello." His arrogant tone pissed me off.

"Put Amelia back on the phone," I demanded, rolling my neck like he was in front of me.

"No," was his icy response.

"Who are you?" The agitation in my question was front and center.

"The name is Nasir."

Finally got a name out of him. I repeated it under my breath. "Nasir, leave my friend alone,"

I heard Amelia yell out.

"Tell your friend she needs to call you back. We're having lunch," Nasir stated.

"Listen here—" Never had I had to deal with a person this combative. I wasn't sure how much Amelia had told him, but he needed to understand I didn't play childish games.

"Sorry, Cyrah," Amelia muttered over the call.

I leaned against the wall in the trailer. "Who the hell is Nasir?" I planted a hand on my hip.

"He's my coworker and friend when he's not an asshole," Amelia said.

I smirked when I heard him argue back. "Well, I'm happy you called."

"Me too. I heard you were in the hospital." Amelia sounded sad.

"Cyrah, you know your mom is going to curse me out," Tanja hissed, looking out the trailer window.

Sable really would curse her out. Everyone on set had complained about how she tried to run things because I had a producing credit on my projects. "Stop being scared, Tanja."

Tanja shifted from one foot to the other.

"Amelia, can I call you back?" One thing I prioritized was not being a diva by holding up the cast and crew for selfish reasons.

"Can we get together for lunch this week?"

"Sure. Send me a text with the address of the location." I switched back to the vanity to get done up.

"How much longer are you planning on being on the

phone?" Nasir asked in the background.

"Why does he care?" I shouted.

Amelia laughed at me. "Stop it, Nasir!" The line went dead.

"Jerk." I clicked off and dropped the phone in my purse.

"What's wrong with you?" Tanja wondered, tilting my head up and forward to get a better position.

"Nothing. Just finish with my hair so I can get out of here."

It was crazy how that voice sounded familiar and irritated me. Between my mother and the guy on the phone, I needed to go on vacation. I had bags under my eyes, and I needed to be away from work for a little while and regroup before I planned my next project.

Sable Brinkley had already tried to fill my schedule with interviews and hosting gigs, but I'd been able to tell Mikka to block out a week for me to do nothing. It was embarrassing to end up in the emergency room from dehydration and exhaustion. To see myself this vulnerable was hard on top of losing a little weight off my thick frame.

"Showtime, Cyrah," Tanja reminded me.

I puckered my lips and smiled in the mirror. "Thanks, Tanja."

I went to the trailer door, pushed it open, and saw the PA arrive in the golf cart to take me to set.

"Everybody ready, Luthor?" I climbed into the cart and lifted the script off the seat.

"Yep, all ready for you," Luthor replied.

"Good. We can get this day over with."

The script had been rewritten with a few new scenes with different colored highlights.

Luthor stopped in front of the studio lot for my new film, *Descent into Lies*. I thanked him and sauntered inside to run through lines with the script coordinator as the lighting was adjusted.

―――――

"Sable, I'm taking some time off because I need a break." I walked out of my spa room in my house with my face mask on and held the phone up to my ear. I'd finished filming last night, slept like a baby, then arranged for my esthetician to make a house call and work on my self-care today.

"You know anyone can take your place while you're on vacation," she pointed out.

I walked into my kitchen to see my chef cooking break-fast. "No one can take my place. You raised me to know better," I argued, lifting the water jug. I poured a glass and sat at the kitchen table.

"I have too much planned out for you to get lazy, Cyrah." As my mother, you'd think she would speak posi-tively to me, but Sable's mindset refused to be nurturing.

"How am I lazy?" A pile of magazines sat on the top. Sometimes I'd have Mikka pick them up for me so if I my name was mentioned, I'd be able to get on top of any gossip or misinformation.

"Are you getting an attitude with me?" Sable snapped.

Her ego wouldn't calm down for a second, even when talking to her own daughter.

Bleep! Bleep!

"I have another call. Let me get back to you."

"Don't you dare hang up on me," Sable barked.

I ignored her statement and clicked over to Amelia's call. I winced slightly, but tuned out my mom's words and returned to my old friend, interrupting our call.

"Can you please tell me if you are free this week, Amelia?" I pulled my bottom lip into my mouth.

"Depends."

"On what?" Fed up with the entire week, I'd probably agree to anything.

"If you don't mind coming to me," she answered nervously.

"What do you mean?" My stomach growled, and I ran a hand over it.

"Well, I still need to finish up some work, and then we can go out for lunch."

"Oh, well, how much time do you need?" I looked at the time on my watch. It was almost noon.

"Maybe thirty minutes, then I'll be all yours, and we could have drinks," Amelia suggested.

"Sure, I can come to you."

"Great, it's TN Security Services on Popular and Clinton."

"Your job sounds complicated just by the name." I tossed the trash magazine away and got off the stool to go change.

"I love it, honestly, but you can come through the back employee entrance if that makes it better."

"I'll have my driver pick you up. I plan on relaxing today."

Nine times out of ten, I used a driver because it could get a little overwhelming when I tried to go places. Fans tended to hound me nonstop and wanted pictures when I didn't look my best.

"I forgot the perks of being a celebrity." Amelia giggled.

I smiled. "Can you believe we haven't seen each other in so long?"

"How long are you here in Chicago?"

"About four months because of filming." If everything went well in LA, I could use this as another resume boost for a bigger role that stripped all the glamor away like Halle and Charlize did when they won Oscars.

"Then back to Hollywood?"

"Yes, my mom booked another project with me as producer and actress."

"Sounds exciting."

"Very exciting, but I need to call her back because I hung up on her to talk to you."

She gasped. "No, you didn't."

"I did, so when she curses me out, I'll blame it on you," I joked.

Amelia knew how my mom was growing up back in the day when we all lived in the same neighborhood in Kenwood. I'd always aspired to be an actress, and with my mother's help, I accomplished my goals. Not that my father wasn't happy with my career later on when I was more established. But he didn't see it as a real profession and had higher expectations of me attending college and getting a real job.

"Hello, Sable."

"The next time you hang up on me, find yourself a new manager," Sable suggested.

I knew she was pissed I hadn't given in to her demands from earlier. "Where's Dad?" I sipped on the water.

"Out golfing."

The golf club he belonged to held a lot of high-profile members, a lounge, a pro shop, and tournaments where the biggest golfers played. He had something that kept him busy and brought him happiness.

"Ever since he retired, all he does is golf."

"Your father worked hard to give us a good life. He deserves to enjoy himself."

"So I'm the breadwinner. You know what, change the subject."

"Are you calling to change your mind about the interviews?" she asked, ignoring my complaints.

"No, I'm about to hang with Amelia."

My everyday clothes were labeled with pictures on the outside with the date I'd worn them, so I wasn't caught in the same look again. My biggest request was the walk-in closet, and I'd hired someone to organize everything along with Mikka. It also held the potential makeup looks that went well for the day, even if the weather was off.

"Who?"

"Amelia, my friend from the old neighborhood."

"I don't know who that is, Cyrah, but you can't be out around just anyone."

"She's not just anyone," I grumbled, looking at the time on the clock on the wall.

"What if a photographer gets a shot of you walking around with someone not in your lane?"

"Sable, stop being dramatic."

"As your manager, I have to think of these things."

"Why did I call you back?" I muttered to myself as I bent down to face different heels in front of the mirror against my foot.

"Because you know I'm right. Get some sleep and call me back when you have your mind straight."

"Tell Dad I said hello." I quickly ended the call and sat back in the kitchen chair, pushing the plate out of my way.

Steward Brinkley avoided all events to do with me and the public life. As soon as I hit it big, he retired from his executive position at the light company. Credit was due to my parents because of the structure in my life, but it brought more confusion when I wanted to be a normal kid and hang out with my friends. Amelia was the one consistent friend in my life before we went our separate ways, with me doing auditions and her being more involved in high school activities.

I finished washing off the facial mask, pulled my hair out of the ponytail, and fluffed it out from the curls yesterday. I came out of the bathroom, removed the gray and white jumpsuit off the hanger, and put it on, zipping the front. I angled left then right at my figure and smoothed my hands down my sides, releasing a soothing breath and anxiety from the phone call with my mother. *Ignore her words,* I repeated to myself as I lifted the black heels, placed them on my feet, and slid on my favorite bracelet. I picked up my black shades and purse to finally have a day of fun with an old friend.

Amelia would be ready for drinks as soon as we got to the restaurant. I had a light breakfast, so I was starving, but I needed to not overdo it with me filming, and some of them involved love scenes.

After getting to the door and waving to some of my garden staff, I climbed into the backseat of the Tesla and gave the address of the company Amelia had given me through text message.

"Ma'am, do you need to have security with you?"

"No, why?"

"I received a text from your mother." Claude raised his phone to show me.

Mrs. Sable Brinkley: *Claude, make sure she has security at all times.*

"Reply with I'm fine."

"Are you sure?" Claude hesitated.

"Yes, she just wants to control everything."

Claude had been with me for the last three years.

"Of course, ma'am." He stopped at the light and replied to her text. The light changed to green, and he turned right for the main street.

I went to my social media, reshared a few comments praising my performance in *Rush into Love* and deleted a few hateful statements.

"Either they hate you or love you." I kissed my teeth, saw the trending news in America, and closed right out. It was beyond ridiculous, and I wouldn't let it ruin my day.

"We've arrived, ma'am."

I looked out the window at a tall building that looked like a factory or, more so, a prison.

"Are we sure this is the place?"

"Yes, the address came up. This is it."

"All right. Wait for me. I shouldn't be long." I opened the door and climbed out, walking to the private employee area, and hitting the buzzer.

"Can I help you?" A voice asked.

I looked around the door to find an intercom. "Uh, yes, I'm trying to get in."

"You're supposed to go through the front for client appointments."

"Well, I'm not a client, my friend—"

"I don't care. You need to come through the front."

I swallowed hard as a tangle of words stuck in my throat. "Are you always this rude?" Every person I'd encountered that Amelia worked with or hung around seemed terrible.

"When people I don't know show up to my business without notice."

"Who am I speaking with?"

He dismissed my earlier comment. "Why?"

I looked around the silver gated door, then up to the top, and saw a small camera focused on me. He was watching me right now and thought he could intimidate me.

"I need to speak with the manager. I'm Cyrah Brinkley, and you're making a big mistake."

"Really? Trying to pull that card again." Rustling could be heard in the background.

"Wait a minute. I know that voice."

This was the asshole who'd interrupted my call with Amelia the other day, and now he was on a roll to get under my skin. I puffed out my chest. Claude stood near the car, and I knew he wanted to come over and see what the problem could be.

CHAPTER 3

Nasir

"HOW MUCH LONGER ARE YOU going to play this game?" Nicco inquired as I hovered over his desk and spoke into the monitor.

He'd noticed when the car arrived and she stepped that something was familiar about her and told me to come and check it out. I would never forget her face as long as I had breath because it was like an annoying bird always chirping.

Buzz! Buzz!

"Be nice," Nicco said.

I watched Amelia open the door. "She's the reason we're still dealing with the fallout from the hospital," I snorted and scratched the top of my head.

Amelia and Cyrah hugged and walked to her office.

Nicco nodded. "Understandable, but Aydin won't let you upset Amelia."

"We'll see about that."

I marched down the hall to Amelia's office, not waiting for permission before barging inside. Something about Cyrah's attitude annoyed the fuck out of me. She seemed to think all the little people should accommodate her needs before anyone else.

"Amelia, he's an asshole," Cyrah hissed. Her back was to me, and Amelia thought it was amusing as my jaw dropped in aggravation.

"Better to be an asshole than a brat."

Cyrah turned at my voice. "Get out." She pointed toward the door.

When her car had pulled up and she'd gotten out of the back, I knew she was used to getting her way. She was still wearing her shades, and Amelia was probably about to go hang out with her and talk nothing but crap about me.

"You have some nerve." I got in her face.

"Nasir, be nice." Amelia jumped up and stepped in between us.

I'd never hit a woman. I might curse them out, but abuse was never a thing the Crowne men did. I gave credit to my dad and aunt for raising me with respect even though my mother bailed on us. Amelia had nothing to worry about with Cyrah and me.

"Nasir, huh?" Cyrah folded her arms against her chest.

"Yeah, Cyrah *brat* Brinkley." The name came sour against my tongue.

"What the hell is your problem?" Cyrah poked me in the chest.

"You cost my team a job," I snarled.

"Nasir, that is not fair," Amelia said, shaking her head in annoyance.

I knew she was right, but Cyrah rubbed me the wrong way, despite her beauty. I admired Cyrah, from her long legs, skinny jeans, and open-toe pink heels. Her jacket barely covered her full breasts and curvy waist. She was sexy, and I hated that I was attracted to her inviting smile, high cheekbones, and oval-shaped eyes.

"Not fair is her having the hospital blocked off, which held up my job," I pointed out.

"Hospital," she murmured. Her eyes went wide, and she snapped her fingers.

"Now you remember behaving like a child at the hospital," I said sarcastically.

"Nasir!" Amelia scolded.

Cyrah stepped around Amelia and got back in my face. "Repeat what you said."

"Nasir, is there a problem?" Aydin's voice filled the room.

It was his business, and I'd let Cyrah's attitude turn me into someone I didn't like.

"No problem at all. Sorry, Amelia." I shifted around Cyrah and left the office.

———

"What was that back there?" Aydin shut the door of my office.

"Nothing." I closed my eyes for a brief second.

"She got under your skin." If anyone understood my dilemma, Aydin should.

"That was the woman I told you about from the shooting."

"Amelia's best friend from childhood?" Aydin probed.

"Amelia needs better friends," I responded.

I'd allowed Cyrah to get under my skin. She probably thought any man would fall at her feet. Well, Cyrah Brinkley had met her match because I didn't sugarcoat anything. I never disrespected a woman, but Cyrah was stuck up, annoying, and thought the world should grovel at her feet.

"Before you cause even more of a dust-up between my

wife and me, the situation with the sniper needs to be resolved." Aydin gave me an intense stare.

"Did they get any updates?" Most security jobs would end in a day after an event, the client would be safe, and all we'd have to do is paperwork. Hearing about a sniper made me more agitated in our lack of movement as a team.

"They have an address for a suspect." Aydin dropped the papers on my desk.

"Zander Rhodes, former sniper and special ops," I read off the document.

"Trained assassin."

I frowned. "What's the connection?"

Governor Johns was like any other politician, but to get on the radar of a trained assassin is huge.

"Seems like our governor was not completely truthful with us about a few things."

"How bad is it for us?"

Aydin stood behind the chair. "Enough that we not only need to find this person but they might have a connection to your little friend."

"Aydin, either you're fucking with me, or you're telling me Cyrah Brinkley is not going away so easily."

"Cyrah Brinkley is not going away, Nasir, and you are going to ensure she's protected."

"What?" I jumped out of my seat, disapproval evident in my voice.

"I need to confirm some things, but it seems Zander Rhodes shot the French president as a decoy. He wanted to get the governor and Cyrah." Aydin's brow curved into a deep frown.

"Kill two birds at once. This is nuts."

I would always agree to a job that would help us catch the enemy fast, but Cyrah Brinkley would not be an easy task.

"Cyrah has a stalker."

"Where is he?" All of my questions probably had him more frustrated than me, as the media put out they were under our company's security.

"No one knows," Aydin answered.

"Cyrah hasn't said anything." My legs felt frozen in place.

"That's where you come in." He rocked on his heels.

I held my hands up to stop him. "Not getting involved. Get Jasper or Nicco." I took an involuntary step back.

"Too late. You've made contact." He blinked with slow purpose and squared his shoulders.

"No, Aydin." The ache in my chest threatened to explode.

"Sorry, brother, this is our job."

"Shit, I need a drink." I scanned the stack of documents on my desk.

Today's weather forecast was sunny and breezy, but I felt a storm brewing. My entire day had gone downhill with his revelations.

"Already spoke with the governor's assistant, and you have an appointment with him."

"Let me guess, right now."

"And please don't get yourself kicked out." A squint crinkled the corners of Aydin's eyes.

I yanked the office door open and marched down to Amelia's, but it was empty. Molly walked by, and I reached for her. "Where did Amelia go?"

"Out," Molly replied, shifting the stack of printed papers to her right hand.

There was no point in going back and forth with Molly on the subject. Amelia was in danger, and Cyrah needed to stay away from her until we found this guy. My only goal was to question the governor, find out who Cyrah's ex was, and get things back to normal.

———

At the front of the governor's office, I waited for the assistant to let me know it was time to go inside. She'd informed me he was on back-to-back calls, and today was busy for him. Nicco and Jasper had tagged along with me while I put Vaughn in charge of finding out more about Cyrah Brinkley.

Tera put the phone down and waved me to go in. "He has about ten minutes of free time."

"I only need five." I cracked my knuckles.

Nicco planted a hand on my chest. "This is the governor, no matter what."

I nodded. Our team knew I stayed calm, but when my intelligence was being played with, I put an end to the problem as soon as I found out what had disturbed my peace. "He's safe for now."

The governor shook my hand and sat back in his chair, twirling his pen. "Nasir, I didn't know we had a meeting today. I thought you had all the information sent over from my team."

"Do you know a Zander Rhodes?" I didn't hold my tongue. He was the same as any other client when we needed answers.

"Who?" He squinted his eyes, sitting forward in his chair.

"Zander Rhodes."

"Not familiar with that person."

"How is the French president doing?" I studied his body language to see if he'd give any clue if he were behind anything from the other night.

"Still recovering but doing well. As a matter of fact, I want to throw a celebration party in his honor and would like your team to work it that night." He wrote something on a piece of paper and passed it to me.

I scanned it to see an address and contact name.

"That's the party planner and address of where we'll have the party," the Governor said.

"Can you remember anything of that night? Like if anyone was forceful about approaching you?"

"I haven't been the most graceful governor since I came in three years ago, but with my election coming up and this incident…"

"Your numbers have gone up."

He shrugged, stood from his chair, slid his hands in his pockets, and angled around his desk. "I don't look at numbers. This was a tragedy, and everyone involved needs to heal."

"This wasn't an isolated incident."

"As governor, threats come and go. You can check the voicemail messages I have Tera check before I hear them. Nothing new." He chuckled and unlocked the door for me to leave. "Call my assistant once you meet with your team."

"One last time, is there anything I should know before I leave?" I stared at him while he avoided eye contact and simply smiled.

"Nothing to hide." He did his best to stifle a grin.

I stuck my hand out for a shake. "See you soon, Governor."

Politicians were all alike, and he wasn't the first to have skeletons in his closet. Our problem was that he'd likely try to pin it on our lack of proper training or some other bullshit to get out of any legal issues from the president's shooting.

Nicco made his way out of the building. I opened the passenger door, and he ducked into the back seat.

"He's behind this," Nicco said, referring to the governor.

"People like him always show their true colors."

Jasper started the car and drove out of the building,

heading to the construction site of Zander's last known employment.

Buzz!

I glanced down at the vibrating phone to see Amelia's name.

lilsisAmelia: You need to apologize.

Me: Never happening.

lilsisAmelia: I thought you were a good guy.

Me: She's bad news.

lilsisAmelia: Leave my friend alone, Nasir.

Me: Sorry, I can't do that.

lilsisAmelia: I'm telling Aydin.

Jasper stopped in front of a lot under construction with a big sign that read *Coastal Rentals Coming Soon*. After the car turned off, I jumped out, and Nicco took a picture of the area with his phone.

"Can I help you?" An older guy with a hard hat, green vest, a large round belly, and a thin mustache approached us.

"Does Zander Rhodes still work here?"

He removed his hat and tucked it under his arm. "I haven't heard that name in about a year," he mused to himself.

"So he did work here?"

"A while back, yeah." He wiped a hand over his mouth.

"How was he?"

To work up a report on him, we needed to know everything from how long he took on a break to the people he hung out with during the shifts. All these guys became family after a few years together.

"In the beginning, he was fine, but last year he only came in when he felt like it. Then one day, he just decided not to show up."

I reached in my pocket to pull out my business card and

handed it over to him. "Call me if you hear anything else or if he makes contact with you."

"Is he in trouble or something?"

"No, I just need to confirm something with him," I lied, trying not to reveal the real reason we were here. The guy could still be in touch with him and tip him off, and I'd hate to come back and send him to the same place I planned on sending Zander.

"Time to go," Nicco said and went to the car.

Amelia texting me had given me an idea. "Before we go to another address, let me call to get the location on Amelia."

"She's going to curse you out." After Nicco adjusted his seatbelt, he pushed the windows down.

"I'm her favorite person."

He chuckled, started the car, and pulled out of the area.

"Yes, Nasir." Amelia sounded annoyed with me. Our relationship was like brother and sister. She'd tried many times to invite me out with her and Aydin on double dates, but I'd declined. Now it was my turn to get on her nerves.

"Where are you?" I checked the time on my watch.

"Why?" Amelia never questioned it when asked about her whereabouts.

"Because I have a gift for you." The only time Amelia fell for any of my older brother routines is when I brought her something to work.

Nicco and Jasper laughed at me lying to get into her good graces.

"Is Nicco laughing in the background?" Amelia caught on.

I held my finger up to my lips for them to be quiet. "No. Aydin told me to drop a gift off to you since I'm on a location scout, a new assignment we have."

"He didn't tell me about a new assignment," Amelia commented.

I knew our conversation would get sidetracked unless I changed the subject. "Amelia, do you want the gift or not?"

I glanced at Nicco, who was about to turn toward the freeway.

"All right, Nasir, but you need to be nice to my friend when you get here."

"I'm a nice guy." I played it off.

"Ha! That's a lie," a voice yelled in the background.

"Cyrah, be nice, please," Amelia fussed.

Cyrah's comment only made me more ready to burst her bubble when I saw her again. I heard whispering back and forth over the phone. Cyrah's drama from earlier stayed on my mind.

"We're at the Vienna bar and restaurant," Amelia remarked.

I gave the location to Nicco and hung up, not waiting for a reply from Amelia.

"That's not far from here on the freeway." Nicco switched lanes and turned at the light to make a U-turn back the way we'd come.

Honk!

The driver in the car behind us blew his horn as Nicco cut him off, causing him to miss the light. Enough was happening with Cyrah, the governor, and Zander. To end up in a car accident was the late thing I needed on our plate.

CHAPTER 4
Nasir

"THIS IS a restaurant and Amelia's friend. Try not to cause a bigger problem." Nicco said, trying to look out for my relationship with Amelia.

When I called her li'l sister, I meant it. I also thought of Aydin and the rest of the guys as my brothers. As an only child, I'd grown up with my dad because my mom ran off when I was seven to be free of any responsibilities.

When I was in high school, she returned for a few days, pretending she cared about me, and I'd fallen for the bull-shit. One of the reasons my father wanted me to go in the Navy was because of my temper. I was always getting into fights, getting kicked out of school, or skipping. He thought it was best for his son to get structure and guidance. Every day I'm grateful to have him as my father, best friend, and the only person who could check me besides Aydin and Amelia.

"Sis, sorry to bug your little lunch date." I bent down and kissed Amelia's forehead, then pulled on her hair.

"Where's my gift?" Amelia held out her hand.

I gave her a high-five. "Sorry, I left it at the office," I lied.

She scoffed, trying to slap me on the chest.

"I was having a good time before he came." Cyrah picked up her martini glass and locked her bow-shaped red lips around the glass.

I shook the thought of her lips sucking on my tongue out of my head and cleared my throat. "We need to talk." I pointed at her.

"I have nothing to say to you." Cyrah sat up straight in her seat and flicked her hand in a dismissing motion.

"Based on the information I just received, we have a lot to talk about."

"What's going on, Nasir? Is this the job you were talking about?" Amelia could help Cyrah to understand that she was in terrible danger.

"Yeah, she's my next assignment."

Cyrah spat out her drink. She picked up a napkin to wipe her chest and the table from her spill. "Assignment? I don't know what you're talking about, but we have nothing that involves us two being around each other."

"It's not easy for me either, lady, but you have to be under my protection until we can find your ex-boyfriend."

"My ex? I haven't spoken to him in years, and I have no plans to."

Trying to get her to listen was going to be harder than I'd expected. Maybe if I apologized, it would show I was serious. "That may be true, but until I can find the guy who tried to kill you, we will be around each other."

"Amelia, your friend is crazy."

"Cyrah, listen to him." Amelia covered Cyrah's hand on the table to make her understand this was a serious situation.

"I have no clue what he's talking about." Cyrah seemed agitated. If she wanted to handle things without us, I was more than happy to have someone else lead the case.

Pop! Pop!

Everyone in the restaurant dropped to the floor. I dove over the table to cover Cyrah as Nicco grabbed Amelia and pulled her down.

"Arghh! Arghhh! Call the police!" Cyrah screamed, trying to run toward the back.

I jumped up and chased her through the hallway.

Ratttaaa! Ratttaa!

"Get down!" I engulfed her beneath me and covered her head.

"Please, get me out of here!" Cyrah cried, trembling in my hold.

"You're safe. It's all right," I whispered in her ear.

The shooting finally stopped, and we heard sirens. I jumped up, and Cyrah gripped my hand.

"Wait, don't leave me. Please, don't go."

"I'll be right back. I need to check on Amelia." I gave her my reassurance before walking from the hallway. I saw broken glass, a few people who were hurt, and EMTs starting to assist them.

"Amelia, you good?" Nicco helped her up from the floor.

"Is Cyrah all right?" Amelia wobbled back and forth.

I helped her to sit. "You might have a concussion. Take a seat." My arms tightened around her. "You're not going anywhere."

"I'm okay, guys. Check on Cyrah." Amelia brushed a hand over her arms.

"Aydin's on the phone," Jasper said, holding the phone out for me to take.

"Let the EMTs help you, Amelia." I started to go back to Cyrah.

"Nasir!" Aydin shouted from the phone.

"Amelia's fine," I assured him.

Cyrah was sitting with another EMT when I approached.

"Cyrah Brinkley! Cyrah Brinkley!" A group of fans and photographers stood outside the restaurant, yelling for her attention.

"Can we get them out of here?" I barked and went to stand by Cyrah.

"What the fuck is going on? Amelia's not answering my call," Aydin spat.

"She's with an EMT, and police are roaming, on top of photographers. The place is probably blocked off."

"If my wife is there, I'm coming in to get her," Aydin barked.

I glanced at Cyrah when she winced under the medic's bright flashlight.

"I'll be there soon." Aydin hung up. Nothing would keep him away.

"How is she?" I questioned as the medic finished his exam.

"She's in shock, but no bruises. I advise her to go to the hospital."

"No, I'm fine, really," Cyrah objected.

"Maybe you should go," I replied.

"And have all the photographers print gossip about me, causing me to lose out on roles?" Cyrah argued.

My mouth hung open. "You care more about what they say than getting help, lady?"

"The name is Cyrah, not *lady*."

"Cyrah! Cyrah! Oh, thank God, you're not hurt." The woman from the hospital—her mother, I assumed—hurried over and hugged her.

Cyrah waved off the medic when he tried to offer her a ride to the hospital. "Sable, you're squeezing too hard."

Cyrah's mom released her.

"We aren't finished talking." I interrupted their conversation.

"You! Did he do this?" Sable demanded.

Cyrah looked at her mom in confusion. "What? No."

"Cyrah, be quiet. You're not thinking clearly. This man was at the hospital yelling in your face, and now he's at the same restaurant as you when bullets start flying around," Sable yelled as police started to come.

"Lady, you're barking up the wrong tree," I snapped.

She held a hand to her chest. "Officer! He's hurt my daughter," she shouted, blocking Cyrah from me.

"Sable, hush and stop lying," Cyrah growled.

"You have a reputation to protect, and this is the second time this man has been around when something bad happened," her mother lied.

"Mrs. Brinkley, Nasir is a friend of mine." Amelia walked over to calm the situation.

"I warned her about being around you, and now I can see the type of people she surrounds herself with because he's crazy," Sable hissed.

I clenched my jaw when I felt a pat on my back.

"Aydin is coming," Nicco shouted, and everyone turned to the door being yanked open.

"Amelia!" Aydin jogged to her, lifted her in his arms, placed her back on her feet, and checked her face for injuries.

"I'm fine, Aydin." Amelia rubbed her hands on her thighs.

"Are you sure?" Aydin queried, angling her around and then back to face him.

"I'm taking my daughter home. Can you please excuse us?" Sable demanded.

"I need your number," I said.

"Why?" Cyrah and her mom asked at the same time.

"Because we have unfinished business."

Cyrah was hesitant, looking from me to Amelia for confirmation. She finally took the phone out of my hand and stored her number.

"Cyrah, you are not dealing with that man," Sable whispered in her ear.

She fussed as they were both escorted out of the restaurant to reporters and fans mobbing her for autographs and pictures.

Later that night, while giving my statement on today's shootout, I visited my dad for our usual Thursday family dinner. He pushed a bottle of beer to me and popped the top off.

"What did you cook?"

"You know your father couldn't compete with my baked Tuscan chicken, three-bean salad, and yams." Aunt Faye ran down the menu, wiping a hand on her apron.

All I could do was smile because they'd both told me they'd grown up fighting like cats and dogs but wouldn't let anyone else insult the other. My aunt's husband, Roy, had died a few years ago, and her daughter, Kelis, was away at college. They still lived close to each other, so going from my dad's house to Faye's, I was grateful for the support.

"Hush that noise, Faye," Dad grumbled, focusing on the basketball game.

He'd retired from working for the city. Being the son of a garbage truck driver in the city often got me teased, but I appreciated him and the many talks he'd given me about a man doing an honest job to feed his family.

"Oh, shut up, Drummond." Aunt Faye smacked him on the back of the head.

Dad rubbed the sore spot, and I chuckled. "She's driving me crazy," he grumbled.

"That's your sister," I joked, stretching my arms out on the back of the couch.

"When are you going to bring a woman home for us to meet?" Aunt Faye brought plates out and put them on the table.

"Never." I reached for the fork, and she slapped my hand.

"Then you don't eat." Aunt Faye went to grab the plate from me.

"Come on, Faye. Stop playing."

She popped me on the head and sat down next to me with her plate. "At your big old age, you should be married or dating someone. I want kids running around here," Faye fussed.

"Not interested." This conversation was so old, and she saw my body slump back in the chair.

"Drummond, you need to talk to your son." Aunt Faye's eyes swept me up and down.

"Faye, I'm thirty-five. Pops doesn't run me."

Dad whipped his head around and stared at me. I threw my hands up, and Faye laughed.

"Faye, leave the boy alone," Dad demanded.

Faye grumbled under her breath. "You are not getting old, Drummond, and neither am I. Crowne's legacy needs to carry forward."

"You better adopt a dog," I replied, and she popped me on the back of the head.

"How's work?" Dad asked.

"Still dealing with the aftermath of the shooting."

"How did that even happen? A president was shot." Aunt Faye spoke.

"Something the team is still researching."

"When we saw the news articles, it scared us." Aunt Faye planted her hand on her chest.

"That's my job, Faye." I gave a dismissive shrug.

"Well, your job is dangerous, and I need you to rethink some things."

I reached over and kissed her on the cheek, and she patted my leg.

"Then we hear about a shootout at a restaurant," Aunt Faye remembered, sipping her tea.

"Aunt Faye, you knew my job was dangerous."

"I do, but it scares me, Nas. You're my baby." Aunt Faye rubbed the top of my head and called me by my childhood nickname.

"Don't let your daughter know," I joked.

She waved me off. "Leave my baby out of this."

Aunt Faye was the closest thing I had to a mother figure in my life, and my cousin, Kelis, had always supported our relationship. If something happened at school and my dad couldn't make it, Aunt Faye would show up.

"Is she coming down for a visit?" I wondered about my little cousin.

"She was here about a month ago. I need to call and see when she can come back," Aunt Faye answered.

I stood, dropped my fork on the plate, and headed to the kitchen. I finished my drink and washed my plate.

"All right, old folks, I'm out." I came out of the kitchen, slapped hands with my dad, and bent down to hug my aunt. I had an early meeting to go over my case.

"Call me old again and see what happens." Aunt Faye pretended to throw punches, and I dodged them and laughed.

"Be good, woman," I called out, shut the door of his house, and headed to my car.

I only lived about thirty minutes away and made it home around eight-thirty. I headed into my townhouse and locked the door. Dropping my keys in the crystal bowl, I removed my shirt and shoes and headed to the shower. After I lifted the hamper to put my dirty clothes in, I grabbed a fresh towel and turned the faucet on to brush my teeth.

Ring! Ring!

I looked out of the bathroom and saw the phone ringing on the dresser. I strolled over to pick it up and saw Aydin calling.

"What's up?" I sat on the edge of the bed, leaning back to stare at the ceiling.

"The shootout was for Cyrah today," he muttered.

"I had a feeling." All of my antennas were up at this news.

"She's not your favorite, but you need to get on board with her," he said with a sigh.

"I got you, Aydin." I absentmindedly cracked my knuckles.

"Did you meet with the governor?" He sounded exhausted. The entire team had worked around the clock after the restaurant shooting.

"No, I got distracted with the shooting, then I met with my folks for dinner."

"Are you able to handle this case?" He was always frank in tone when he felt something could be over-whelming for one of the guys on a mission.

"Aydin, you know me. I can handle it and her."

"Have a conversation with her, then find out if she has any enemies." He probably doubted that I could separate our fighting back and forth, but at the end of the day, if someone needed help, that was a priority, no matter how I felt about them personally.

"I'll see you at the office. Is Amelia good?" I inquired.

"A little shaken up, but I got her relaxed now."

"Tell her I'll bring her favorite cookies tomorrow."

"She'll love that."

"Cool, talk to you at the office." The mention of Amelia and her still dealing with the anxiety from the shootout, plus the past events she'd had to deal with, would put her back in a bad place. I plugged my phone in and closed a few apps when an article about Cyrah Brinkley popped up.

Cyrah Brinkley to star in a new TV project in Los Angeles.

I read the words, shook my head, and went back to get ready for bed.

CHAPTER 5

Cyrah

BEFORE THE SHOOTING.

"Amelia, he's a fucking jerk." I snatched my shades off, removed my jacket, and sat across from Amelia at the restaurant as the waitress came over to take our drink orders.

"I'm so sorry, but I'm a huge fan of yours, Miss Brinkley." The waitress didn't bother being professional at all.

"Thank you, Heather. Do you mind taking my order, please?"

I cut to the chase, read the name tag, and Amelia's eyes hiked wide in surprise. Should I have been nicer? Probably, but Nasir had pissed me off, and I was not in the mood to be hounded.

"So sorry. Can I get your drink order?" Heather finally got her act together.

"I'll have an apple spritzer and champagne." After I explained my order, I closed the drink menu.

"And for you?" Heather turned to Amelia.

"The same, please," Amelia responded, holding back her laugh.

"Are you ready to order food?" Heather questioned.

"A salad with the dressing on the side," I replied, not wanting to get too full.

"A burger and fries for me," Amelia answered.

Heather gripped both menus and strolled away to grab our drinks.

"I admire you for being able to eat a burger and fries." I fixed my ponytail and took a piece of gum out of my purse. A few women noticed me and waved, and I put on my movie star smile and waved back.

"You look amazing. Stop worrying about trying to be in the Hollywood mindset of perfection."

"Don't tell that to Sable Brinkley. She would put soap in your mouth." We laughed at my joke, which held truth to some degree.

Heather placed our drinks on the table.

"So, how is being a celebrity for you?" Amelia inquired.

"No more privacy, men are still assholes, but the money is fabulous." I smiled.

"I was trying to avoid a love life myself, but Aydin came along and changed my mind."

"Too busy to date. After my ex and his craziness, I decided to be single and focus on my career."

Heather arrived at the table with our salads. I grabbed my napkin to cover my lap, and Amelia picked up the ketchup for her fries. A double cheeseburger and fries looked good on her plate and fresh. I might end up ordering it to go for a late dinner.

"Aydin seems sweet. Can't say the same for the Nasir guy." When I ate out and ordered salads, I tended to get the dressing on the side to pour because often they'd overdo it and put on too much.

Amelia giggled, and I shrugged. He probably thought I was one those docile women who would fall at his feet, submissive and compliant. Besides his looks, which women probably fawned over, and I could give credit. The dreads did look sexy with the six-four height.

"Nasir is sweet." She took a large bite from her sandwich.

I almost choked on my drink, and Amelia leaned around and patted me on the back. "That man is the devil."

"I think you two would be cute together," she said.

Heather dropped more napkins on the table. Amelia stating that Nasir was cute made me want to gag from the visual. Looks weren't the first thing I went by when dating. I always had to have a personality.

"He's okay." The man was tall, which was a plus, and he came across as the lead alpha in his group. But his personality was nasty.

Amelia cocked her head to the side and grinned at me. "Okay, so you don't notice the wide smile, strong chiseled jawline, thick athletic build, and piercing dark eyes," she teased.

"Never noticed any of that." I took a sip of my drink.

"Stop lying to yourself."

"Sis." The same deep, melodic voice arrived at our table. I sat back in my seat and crossed my hands over my chest in amusement.

"Cyrah! Cyrah!" Sable called my name, drawing me out of the deep sleep from yesterday's events.

I removed the wet towel from the pillow and tossed it on the nightstand as the light in my bedroom turned on.

"What, Sable?" My memory from the restaurant stayed on repeat in my head.

"We need to talk."

"How did you get in here?"

"With my key," Sable answered, sitting in the chair near my window.

I had several homes in Chicago, LA, and New York. As soon as I made it big, I purchased my parents their dream home, got a place for myself, and a condo in the city. Yesterday, I had Claude bring me to my gated home away from prying eyes.

"Sable, I gave you that key for emergencies." I pulled myself up against the headboard.

"This is an emergency. You need to get up. We have things to discuss."

"Did you call the producer and tell them I needed a day or two for myself?"

"Yes, and it's all over the news about the shooting." She shoved the phone in my face.

I rubbed the sleep out of my eyes and scrolled through the articles. "It'll blow over once they find out who shot up the place."

"Well, until they do, you're going to stay away from that girl and her friend."

Ding! Ding!

"Did you invite someone over here?" I reached for my phone and glanced at the security cameras.

"The stylist is here. We need to finalize some of your outfits for LA."

"Sable, today I need to rest. I was in a shooting."

"As your mother and manager, I have to protect you. Your career will only last for so long."

Sable was partially right, even though I made films and did a few guest appearances on TV shows. I had to market myself worldwide and doing different interviews and guest appearances helped to keep my name in the public eye.

Ding!

"Fine. Send—" I jumped out of bed, shocked he'd shown up at my place. I marched down the stairs to give my security team a piece of my mind.

"Cyrah, you cannot answer the door like that!" Sable yelled behind me.

"For once, shut up, Sable!" I turned and yelled from the bottom of the stairs.

"Girl, who are you talking to?" She planted her hands on her hips.

For a second, I forgot she was my mother. We'd never had that special motherly bond. It was always surface, in my eyes. Naturally, she'd worked hard to get me my career, but sometimes I felt it came at the cost of our relationship.

"Sorry, Mommy." I lowered my eyes to the floor like a small child again.

"That's better. Now let Brooks answer the door, and you come and change."

"You don't understand."

Brooks, the house manager, walked out of the living room and headed to the door.

"Cyrah, I'm not telling you again." Her eyes grew darker.

"Just let me talk to Nasir."

"Who?" Sable's head drew back.

"Hello, can I help you?" Brooks unlocked the door and stepped aside to let Shandra in with a suitcase of clothes. Right behind her were Nasir and another guy.

"Brooks, shut the door and call the police!" Mom shouted.

I felt a migraine coming on. Brooks turned toward me, and I nodded to let them inside and directed Shandra upstairs with the clothes.

"I'll be up there in a minute," I said.

Sable came downstairs with the phone to her ear. "He's trespassing." Disapproval gleamed in her eyes.

"Is your mom always like this?" Nasir pointed at her, and his friend laughed.

"What are you doing here?"

"We need to talk." He sighed and watched my mother leave.

"About?" I still felt a little woozy. I needed this conversation to be over quickly, so I could get everyone out of my face.

"Cyrah, security is coming to get him out of here, and I called your lawyer," Sable said.

Nasir let out a harsh breath. "If you want to stay alive, I would cancel that."

"What did you say?" I rested a hand on my hip. Everything was moving too fast for me.

"We showed up at the restaurant to tell you that you're in danger."

"He's lying. Look, I know you're probably starstruck, but my daughter doesn't date broke men," Sable spat.

"Sable, can you make sure my morning breakfast is ready?" I asked, shifting around her to walk into the living room. I motioned for them to take a seat. "First, how did you get my address?" I cut my eyes at Nasir.

"Amelia, but she knows it's life or death." Nasir rubbed his chin.

"I'll call and curse her out for this." Amelia knew I liked to be discreet with my location.

"Actually, you should thank her," his friend said.

"Who are you?" My brows bunched together in confusion.

"Nicco," he answered, and a muscle in his jawline ticked.

All of the media storm from the restaurant, on top of the issues with my mother, plus Nasir coming into my world with his demands, gave me a sinking feeling in my stomach.

"Nicco works with me at the security company with Amelia."

"And?" Everything felt stifling.

"Someone is trying to kill you."

He probably expected me to be grateful, but the security I usually used for red carpet events could handle my safety.

I glanced between both men and burst into laughter. "You're kidding, right?"

They avoid my question.

Neither smiled.

"It's not a joke," Nicco replied.

"No, you were the target of the shootout at the restaurant. The shooting at the playoff game was a decoy. We believe it's all connected." Nasir pinched the bridge of his nose.

"The playoff game."

"Basketball," Nicco replied.

"Sorry, I'm not into sports, have no clue." I shoved a hand through my hair. Suddenly, I felt hot, and my hands were clammy.

"You don't keep up with the news, do you? The French president?" Nasir jammed his hands in his pocket, pulled out his phone, tapped on the screen, and held it up to my face.

"I've been non-stop working on set, and then you involved me in a shootout," I hissed, jumping out of my seat. I spread my hand around his palm to get a better look with the phone closer to my eyes and felt a light shock.

"We're still trying to piece it together. But your ex put out a hit on you." Nasir tucked it back into his pocket.

"Cyrah, here's your food. Come sit down and eat." Sable set the plate on the coffee table.

Food was the last thing on my mind. "That can't be true. He has a temper, but he wouldn't do something like this."

"How well do you know the governor's son?" Nicco probed.

"Well enough to know that he would be stupid to try and have me killed." I took a sharp breath and lifted the top off the food my mother had brought me.

"He's engaged now, correct?" Nasir asked.

"Eric wasn't the best pick for my daughter, but socially it made sense with her career," Sable explained.

"As of right now, you'll need to be under our protection," Nasir stated.

"Under whose authority?" Sable barked.

"Mine." Nasir never looked away, and a cold chill slithered up my spine.

"We believe the French president was a decoy situation to throw us off. They've hired someone to come after you," Nicco explained patiently. He seemed to be the calm one between them. "Do you know any of Eric's secrets?"

Sable glanced at me, then Nasir. I didn't want to be involved in anything regarding the governor and his son's business. Eric would confide in me sometimes, but I tuned most of it out, and to now come to grips with an attempt on my life was too much.

"I don't know anything." I avoided it and scooted back on the couch, covering my face with my hands. The career I'd built up would probably be halted if I got too deeply involved. No more talking about my career, just the alleged assassin trying to kill me. Nasir didn't understand, but no film studio would put money behind me, let alone an insurance company signing off on a project if they thought I was a liability.

"My daughter doesn't need your help." A deep scowl covered Sable's face.

"Starting today, I'll be the head of your security, and Nicco will be second in command," Nasir announced, pointing from himself to Nicco.

I dropped my hands down to my lap, looking up at him. "Why do you care?"

"Because one of my best friends was almost killed, and I never leave a job unfinished." Nasir turned, leaving us alone.

"Oh, my God, this is nuts." I dropped my shoulders and stretched my legs on top of the couch to lie down.

"Maybe we could use this to our advantage." Sable came over, lifted my legs, and sat down to put them on her lap.

Probably too much to think she would drop the manager role for a second and be a mother. There she went, once again mapping out a plan for my career.

I removed my legs from her lap. "I need to be alone for a minute."

"You need to get upstairs and get changed. Shandra is here for two hours, and then we have interviews."

"I told you I was off today." I was over the conversation and stood up.

"Cyrah, you had an incident at a restaurant. This could be big for us." She reached out to grab the plate of food off the table.

"Someone shooting at me isn't an incident, Sable." I fought the urge to throw up at her lack of comfort.

I shook my head and left her in the living room to have a long bath.

———

Nasir and Nicco sat in the front seat while my mother, assistant, and I sat in the back on our way to do a few interviews. She'd hounded me so much I'd given up and decided to get in a few questions because some fans were concerned. Blowing out a deep breath, my mom rambled on about what to stay on topic about and how I should try to cry at the right moment to score a few points with women.

"Amelia knows you're here?" I scooted forward from the back of the black SUV.

"She's at home. Aydin wants her to relax after what happened," Nasir responded.

"Have you spoken with Eric?" I asked.

As I sat in the backseat, Nasir and I made eye contact in the side mirror. Without all the hate in my heart, I could see the prominent cheekbones and sculpted jaw most women went for. Every woman would fall to their knees, but I knew our worlds were too different, and it would never work.

"He's supposedly out of the country," Nicco responded.

"What about his father?" Eric's parents and I never stayed in touch when we were together, let alone after the breakup.

Nicco arrived at the CBG studios, and my mother lowered her window, showing our badges.

"We're watching him to see if he makes contact, but we know you have events coming up that could speed things along faster," Nasir stated.

Already I could see where this question was going. "I don't have time for that with my schedule."

Nicco parked in the reserved spot for the talent, and Nasir shifted in his seat to face me. "The last person who wants to be here is me, but I promised Amelia I would keep you alive, so either get on board or handle it on your own."

Nasir climbed out of the car, came to the back passenger door, and helped us out.

"He's cute." Mikka, my assistant, raked her eyes over his solid body.

"Focus on the job," I snapped.

Placing my hand in Nasir's, I slid out of the SUV, and he steadied a hand on my hip since I was wearing high heels. Our eyes connected briefly, and I remembered I didn't like him. I snatched my hand away, and Julie snickered behind me as Nasir helped her and my mother out.

"Can we get this over with, please?" I sauntered into the studio, greeted by the producer and talent coordinator.

They showed me to the dressing room, and I relaxed in the makeup chair for a touchup. Thankfully, it didn't take long until the show started to air. Nasir and the staff escorted me out of the room to the stage. The audience wrangler got the audience hyped as Enya started the show.

"Ladies and gentlemen, we have the star of *Rush into Love*, Cyrah Brinkley!" the Morning Chicago and Friends host announced.

I smiled, waving at the fans. "Thanks so much for inviting me today, Enya."

We hugged, and I sat across from her on the chair. I always came back to this show on promo tours because it felt like home, and they make sure to keep it fun and fresh every time. Most talk shows were decorated in a business-like manner with no character or style. Enya's show had a home-from-home vibe with a cream, black, and red color scheme. The set was an open space with two chairs, so the audience felt included, and if she had a specific segment like cooking or an artist performing, it stayed within the same color scheme.

"You are one of our favorite guests. You're invited anytime, and your mom," Enya said.

I leaned forward at the audience and pretended to whisper. "Please don't tell her that."

Everyone laughed at my joke.

"I know you're currently filming and have to fly out to LA in a few months." Enya brought fresh energy after the other conversations I'd had lately.

"Yeah, work is hard but a blessing." A warm fuzzy feeling played in my stomach.

"*Daily Magazine* said you're the next Angela, Viola, and Meryl all wrapped into one." Enya's head twisted from me to the audience.

I pretended to fan myself. "No pressure." I looked at the audience and covered my eyes as one of the lights blinded me.

"As you know, it's all over the news about the shooting." Enya wouldn't pass up the chance to bring up the biggest news in the world.

"An unfortunate event, but thankfully, no one was hurt." I crossed my legs and clasped my hands on my knees.

"Can you tell us about what happened?" Enya shifted from one note card to the next, then glanced back at me.

I shifted in my seat, my hands clammy as I looked behind the cameraman to see my mom and Nasir. Why was his presence calming at this moment, even though we clashed constantly?

Leaning over, I grabbed the glass of water and took a sip as all eyes were on me.

CHAPTER 6

Cyrah

"HONESTLY, Enya, it's all a blur to me. I remember dropping to the floor for safety."

This was an ongoing police investigation. I couldn't put more drama on my plate with the authorities.

"From the news articles, you were out for lunch with a friend," Enya continued, squaring her shoulders.

"Yes, one of my childhood friends." A mixture of apprehension and bewilderment started to creep in at the direction of our conversation.

"Do you know why someone would make an attempt on your life?" Enya probed, looking puzzled at my situation.

"No idea. It's disturbing. All I do is focus on my work and family."

Crash!

I jumped in my seat, glancing around the room. Something near the camera light captured my attention.

"The latest project seems interesting."

There was silence in the studio as the audience waited for me to continue. My breath hitched and I blinked rapidly.

"Cyrah."

I heard someone whisper my name.

I cleared my throat. "Sorry, what did you say?"

"I said the latest project looks interesting," Enya repeated with a smile.

I picked up the cup of water, took a sip, and crossed my legs. "A great film with an incredible cast and crew." I gave a basic description to get through the interview.

"Well, it sounds like fun, and I hope you come back when the film wraps. Once again, thank you, Cyrah Brinkley, for coming to hang with us!" Enya announced.

I jumped up and ran over to Nasir and my mom. "Can we go?" I wasn't sure if I was dreaming or just crazy with them hammering Eric down my throat, but it felt like I saw him sitting in the audience.

"You okay?" Nasir placed a hand on my shoulder, looking me over.

I stared at his hand before looking at him. He quickly removed it and cleared his throat.

"What was that, Cyrah?" Sable fussed.

I sauntered out of the studio. "Nothing. I just didn't feel well."

"Then I'll call the doctor, but we can't have you freezing up on camera," she argued.

Nasir pushed me back before he allowed me out.

"No one's going to hurt me here." I moved around him and switched over to the waiting car.

"Cyrah, I have too much lined up for you to fall off now with your career," Mom said.

I slid the door open and paused to turn toward her. I arrowed a glower in her direction. "Is that all you care about?"

She rolled her eyes. "Here you go with that again. I'm your mother and manager. Of course, I care about you." Mom climbed in next to me, and Nasir got in the front seat.

I rubbed my forehead as Mikka got in on the other side of the car. "Do you need an aspirin?" she asked, sliding her hand into her purse. She passed me a bottle of water and pills.

"Thanks." A bad headache was forming, and I needed to cancel the rest of today. Photographers and bloggers would enjoy a headlining report of me slowly losing my mind. "See if you can move the rest of today around."

Nicco started the car and headed through the security gate to the main road.

"The studio is expecting you back on set tomorrow," Sable said, typing on her phone.

"Then push the interviews back to next month."

"Fine, but can you at least do the social media posts?" Sable held back on her anger with the extra people in the car.

She passed me my phone and the printout of what the company wanted me to say. It was a lip gloss company that sent me test samples I promoted for a certain amount. I'd even thought of investing with the company.

"After this, I need a break. Call Tanja and let her know I'll need her tomorrow for set."

The interview wasn't my best, and I'd probably hear about it from agents and studios. When I'd heard the crash of equipment it had startled me. It took me back to the shooting and I was vulnerable again.

Focus on the video promo.

I clicked the video on live with the lip gloss in my hand and smiled. "Babes, I'm here with one of my favorite makeup items I never leave home without. Check them out today because you'll see more of them in the future. Thanks, Gummygloss!"

I blew a kiss, slid the clear gloss across my lips and puckered for the camera. I saw Nasir glance at me at of the corner of my eye. I pushed the gloss back over to Mikka, ended the live show, and gave her the phone to create the hashtags.

"I've emailed Enya to reschedule another interview and to cut that portion where you froze," Sable explained.

Nasir focused on the ride.

"Take me home," I demanded, and he continued the drive out of the studio lot.

Ring! Ring!

"Do you want to talk to Amelia?" Mikka asked.

"Not right now. I need a glass of wine and a hot bath."

"The new script scenes are being delivered," Sable informed me.

"Can you stop talking about work for one second!" I shouted.

Everything went quiet in the car. Usually, I'd prefer us doing work in the car and going over things, so I couldn't fault her, but this wasn't the time to hammer me about what was happening when I needed a moment of peace.

Twenty minutes later, Nasir pulled into my driveway, parked, and came around and open my door. Nicco opened the front door and I sauntered inside toward Brooks, who stood with a glass of white wine ready for me.

"Thank you, Brooks."

"Would you like your food brought up to your room?" Brooks spoke as I headed upstairs.

"Yes, and tell everyone I'm not to be disturbed."

"I need to run over the schedule for tomorrow." Nasir reminded me.

"Tomorrow, I'm on set, so I don't need you around."

"That's not how it works." The corner of his mouth lifted in a sneer.

We had a stare-off.

"Sable will handle my security details with you." I flicked my wrist and continued up the stairs.

Seemed like everyone needed me to do something or be

somewhere. When could I have peace and quiet away from all the bullshit? Having bodyguards around the clock was going to be a disaster. It could make me a liability in the business and cause me to lose jobs. I slammed my bedroom door, plopped down on the top of the bed, and closed my eyes.

"Is Eric really behind the shooting?" I mumbled to myself.

———

The next day I was back on set, running through my lines in my trailer as the hairstylist, Eylana, prepared me for the first scene of the day. Once I'd finished my bath last night and taken a sleeping pill, I was knocked out for the rest of the night and let the past few days drain away.

Eric and I had dated off and on for a year. It was more for publicity on both sides, with him moving in political circles and me wanting to gain a bigger name for myself. It was all constructed by our parents, and at first, I thought it was stupid, but we started to care for each other.

Over time, he became jealous and possessive about every little thing I did, and I would never allow anyone to control me. At first, my mom didn't believe me, and it took him blowing up at a dinner party over me having a conversation with another guy one night for her to finally understand I was done with him.

"I'm going to leave a few curls down." Eylana brushed the ponytail, then picked up the hold spray to complete the look.

"Can you swoop this a little more?" I demonstrated with my hand across my bangs.

"The right side and a little piece down here." She turned my head left, then right to see in the mirror.

"Perfect." I popped my lips twice and checked my teeth.

"You're all set." Eylana put the comb down on the counter and moved to the left of the vanity stand.

"Tanja, can you touch up my lips again?"

Knock! Knock! Knock!

"Who is that?" Tanja called out and sauntered to the door. She pushed the door open, and a wide smile came across her face. "You have a delivery." Tanja beamed.

"From whom?" Everybody closest to me knew I was working and not to be disturbed.

Tanja took the large display of roses, lilies, and sunflowers out of the assistant's hands and placed them on the table before lifting the card off.

"Someone wants to apologize or make a date," Fern teased me.

I took the card and opened it to read it to everyone.

Please forgive me. I can't go through life without you next to me.

I crumpled the card and tossed it in the trash can.

"Who was it from?" Tanja probed.

I hated to put my business out in the open, but I needed to find out how those flowers had gotten so close to me. Nasir had one of his men bring me to the studio today because he had a meeting, but if I had to have protection, I wanted the best at all times.

"Nobody. Secret admirer."

"Are you dating somebody? I remember the governor's son." Tanja peeled off her jacket.

"Just do my makeup, Tanja, please," I barked, dropping the flowers in the trash and sitting back in the chair.

Everyone stood in shock as I forced myself to calm down and not stress,

I picked up the script and continued to read over the changes for the day. "Actually, can you give me a few minutes alone?"

"Um, sure. We will be right outside." Tanja and Eylana walked out.

I grabbed my phone out of my purse and dialed a number I thought I'd erased from my memory.

"You like my flowers?" he asked, and nausea rose in my throat.

"Did you try to have me killed?" I paced back and forth in the trailer.

"I missed you, Cyrah."

"What do you think your father would say about his son tarnishing his name?"

"No one would believe you. We love each other, and you need to stop playing games."

"Eric, listen to me carefully. I don't want you, and I never loved you. It's over. Leave me alone."

"That's going to cost you, sweets."

"Eric!" I yelled into the phone. I removed it from my ear to check the number. I tried to redial, and it disconnected.

The door swung open, and Jasper stepped into the trailer with his gun in his hand. "I heard you yelling. Everything good?"

I threw my head back and rubbed the side of my neck, counting to ten to calm my stress levels. "Yeah. Can you send Tanja and Fern back in, please?" I toyed with my hair and pressed my lips in a straight line.

"I will, but you have to tell me what that call was about." His eyes darted to the flowers in the trash.

I grabbed another lipstick and applied it. "Nothing, just a bill collector."

"Something tells me it wasn't, but I'll leave you to finish, and the flowers in the trash look suspect." Jasper folded his arms over his chest.

"Can you not tell Nasir about this?"

He looked confused. "No. My job is to keep the team informed of everything I see."

"I understand, but it's flowers. Something that small won't help anything." I drew in a long breath.

"My job is to report any news to the team about everything I see and hear," Jasper repeated.

I knew it would only make things even more complicated.

A few hours later, I was finished with filming. I hugged the director and gave some of the crew high-fives as my day was done. Some of the cast wanted to go out for drinks, and I promised to hang with them for a little while before I headed home for the night to go over my lines. Jasper stood at the trailer on watch, and I decided tonight after drinks to try and get things straight with Eric, or at least have his father get him in line.

I preferred to ride with the other actors, so I slipped out of the soundstage and had Tanja grab my things. The wardrobe I had on from my last scene consisted of a long orange, summery dress with short sleeves, and I released a few buttons to show a little cleavage.

"Shouldn't you have your bodyguard with you?" Michael, the co-star of the film, pointed out.

"I'll be fine. It's only a bar, and I don't plan on staying long."

"You should have seen the massive flowers she got delivered today," Tanja said.

My chest tightened at her statement. "Everybody gets flowers. Change the subject."

"Oops, that means it was a man that fucked up," Fatum, another actress, said.

I blew out a breath. "Tonight is not about my life."

Michael pulled up in front of the *R&R* lounge where most of Hollywood hung out on Roberston and Melrose. He handed his key to the valet, and Fatum, Michael, and I all trailed up to the door as the bouncer kept a few fans back.

Smiling, Fatum waved at a few other actors in the lounge and went to talk to them. Michael led the way to a VIP section reserved with bottles of champagne, vodka, and beer. Outside looked like a regular bar with a sign and black door in front, but once you walked inside, it was two stories, over eight thousand feet, with a dance floor. My head bumped to the music from the City Girls as I sat next to Michael, and he poured us a glass.

"Tonight, let's relax and have fun."

I took the drink from him. "Today was long but good," I said, thinking back on our filming.

"If this goes well, I might be able to do a sequel," Michael remarked. He'd played my boyfriend.

"Depending on the reaction from the audience, it could be the next big blockbuster."

Fatum twisted her hips, snapped her fingers, and approached our table. "This is exactly what I needed." She sighed and lifted the bottle of vodka and cranberry juice.

Michael stood. "Come dance with me, Cyrah."

I gave my things to Fatum to hold and followed him. "Not up front. Don't need everybody in our business."

The music changed to nineties house music, and Michael clapped his hands and nudged me on the shoulder. I laughed.

Bump!

"Watch where you're going!" I yelled at the couple behind us.

"Whatever, girl," she spat and rolled her eyes.

"Ugh, can't stand these thirsty groupies."

"What did you say?" She got in my space.

Michael pulled me behind him. "We're trying to have a good time tonight." He held his hands up in prayer.

"She bumped into me," I sassed.

"Girl, you think the world revolves around you or something." The girl tried to reach around Michael, and her boyfriend wrapped his hand around her waist, pulling her back to his chest.

"Do we have a problem?" It was a voice I thought I wouldn't have to deal with tonight.

"What are you doing here?" I stepped around Michael and folded my arms.

"Since you decided to leave without telling Jasper, we tracked you down from social media. You should have told your friends not to post every movement," Darkness crossed Nasir's face.

"Are you her man or something?" The thirsty girl jumped into our conversation.

Nasir grasped my hand and walked me away from them with Michael on my trail.

"Cyrah, who is this?" Michael questioned.

"Her bodyguard," Nasir answered, standing with his chest puffed out.

"Nobody," I replied, stepping in front of him with my back to his chest.

"Jasper is waiting outside. We need to go," Nasir instructed.

I turned my head, staring up at him with a harsh glare. "I don't need your protection here," I snapped, waving my hand around.

"Cyrah, you okay?" Fatum walked up to me.

"Yeah, I need to use the bathroom before I go."

A glance downward at his watch prompted Nasir to turn to Nicco. "Nicco will follow you." He didn't wait for an answer.

"Fatum will come with me, and before you start, keep this from my mother."

"Not in the business of relaying messages between you two," Nasir replied, reaching into his pocket to pull out his wallet.

"Asshole." Despite my uneasy feelings, I grabbed

Fatum's hand, walked into the hallway, and bumped into someone on my way to the bathroom.

"Sorry about that," he apologized. There was something about his presence I couldn't pinpoint.

"No problem." Fatum and I glanced at the guy as he returned to the bar.

"He was kind of cute."

"Men are the last thing on my mind." Once the door was open, I checked the stall and stepped inside to pee.

"So tell me about him." Fatum stood at the mirror, fixing her hair.

I flushed and came out to wash my hands. "Tell you about who?" The water came on as soon as I extended my hand under the faucet.

Fatum turned to look at me as I dried my hands. "The bodyguard." She chewed on her bottom lip and smirked.

"He's nothing." I fluffed out my hair.

"He's fucking hot." She laughed, passed the lipstick back, and I pushed it toward her to keep.

"Fatum, everybody is hot to you." At least once a month, she was tagged in the blogs about who she was dating. I found it incredible she could get to set on time when all she did was party and pose on social media for likes.

"Are you still on a no-dating rule because of Eric?" Fatum took my extra lipstick out to freshen up her look.

I turned left to right in the mirror and checked one last time on my makeup. "Eric is the past."

"Then hop on something new, like the hot bodyguard." Fatum grinned and opened the door right on Nicco and Nasir.

"Can I breathe, for God's sake!" I switched away, grabbing my purse and heading out to the car. Nasir opened the door for me, and I climbed inside.

"If you'd stop running from my team, I wouldn't have to track you down," he barked, getting in behind me.

Jasper started the car, and everyone stayed silent while Nasir tried to scold me like he was my father.

"Your services are no longer needed." As I adjusted in my seat, I pressed my fingers together.

"It's not up to you." Nasir's voice was cocky.

"We'll see about that," I challenged, rolling my neck.

Pop! Pop!

"Get down!" he yelled. He reached across, grabbed me, and covered me on the floor as the car swerved.

"We're being followed," Nicco shouted, and I briefly peeked and saw him reach for his gun.

Pop! Pop!

Glass shattered. Jasper sped up in traffic as cars honked at us.

"Get me out of here!" I shouted with tears falling down my face.

"Cut through here," Nasir demanded.

The car turned suddenly, and jolted like it had scraped a pole.

"Fuck!" Nasir cursed.

It went silent again before I finally removed my hands from my head. Nicco helped me up when the car stopped. Everything was quiet.

"You're fine. We're home." Nicco opened the back door, and Nasir came around and reached for my hand to pull me out. I tightened my hand around his waist.

"It's over. You're safe." Nasir whispered in my ear. He bent and lifted me in his arms bridal style and carried me up the stairs.

"What just happened?" I asked in disbelief, my hands shaking as Brooks pulled open the door.

"Get her something to help her sleep." Nasir tried to release his hold, but I wouldn't let him.

"Where are you going?" My grasp tightened, and I shook my head.

"I need to meet with my team." He covered both of my hands.

"Can't you stay a few more minutes?" Finally, I released my hold on him.

"I'll be right down here." Nasir rubbed my cheek gently.

"I need to call my mom." I closed then opened my eyes, trying to control my breathing,

"Relax for a minute and drink this water." Brooks came out of the kitchen, and I nodded in thanks.

Nicco and Jasper came in, and all three stood together between the entryway and living room, talking while I stayed near. If this was Eric, it wouldn't be easy to keep it out of the media any longer.

Tonight brought back a bad memory of us arguing one day at his place. His flirting had started to affect me and make me look crazy in front of other people. I told him plenty of times, if he was going to cheat, not to make me look stupid.

"Cyrah, you're being dramatic."

"Dramatic! No, Eric. I refuse to let you walk all over me and then cheat in my face."

"No one is cheating." He twirled the glass of Jack Daniels in his hand.

"We had a deal, but I'm done."

I started to leave his bedroom, but he snatched me by my arm. "Listen, you little slut. My father and your mother made a deal."

"Let me go." I tried to jerk out of his hold.

He wrapped both arms around my waist and leaned down to kiss me on the lips, but I angled my head to the left.

"I apologize."

"Too late. You and your family can go to hell."

His grasp tightened, and I winced.

"The day I let you leave me will be the day your mother buries you," Eric seethed, releasing his hold.

I stumbled back and planted a hand on my chest.

CHAPTER 7

Nasir

CYRAH STARED OFF INTO SPACE. I was afraid something like this would happen.

"That was too close." Usually, my senses would be alert, but I'd dropped the ball, and the guilt started to creep up.

"I agree," Jasper answered.

"Did you see anyone following you at the lounge?" I looked over my shoulder at Cyrah in a terrified state. I felt bad about yelling earlier.

"He called me," Cyrah whispered.

"Who?" That had my antennas up.

Her head lifted to make eye contact. "Eric."

"Why didn't you tell me?" We all marched over to her, and I dropped to my knees to hear her better.

"I honestly thought it wasn't him. Even though in the past he was possessive, I didn't think he would do something this serious."

"We need your phone. Anything else?" I extended a hand, and she opened her purse and placed her phone in my palm.

"A guy bumped into me when I went to the bathroom." Cyrah seemed to start remembering her steps.

"How did he look?" I gave Jasper her phone so she could keep talking.

She shrugged. "Normal, about five-ten, dark buzz cut, thin mustache with an athletic frame."

"Could be Zander," Nicco said.

"Who's Zander?" Cyrah wondered, glancing from me to Nicco.

"Did he touch you at all?" I scanned her clothing and homed in on her purse and jacket.

"He grabbed my wrists so I wouldn't fall."

"You think he put a tracker on her?" Nicco remarked. It was a possibility.

Cyrah's eyes rose in suspicion. "Tracker?" She opened her purse and poured everything out.

Nicco reached for her jacket and checked it over with no luck.

"Cyrah!" Sable burst through the door with her father.

"I'm fine." Cyrah stood from the couch and placed her purse on the table.

Nicco and Jasper went back out to check the security cams.

"It's all over the news that you were in a car shootout," Mr. Brinkley said, hugging her tightly.

"We can use this to our advantage," Sable said.

I swallowed hard. Her only child had almost been killed, and she wanted to paint a narrative to boost her career.

"Sable, I don't need this right now." Cyrah moved out of her father's hold.

"Cyrah, think about how the publicity will look tomorrow," Sable urged.

I felt sick to my stomach.

"Sable, not now," her father demanded.

"You haven't even asked how I'm doing." Cyrah pointed at her mother.

Sable grabbed Cyrah's hand and pulled farther away. "Honey, I know you're strong. Don't think I put you above money." She tried to manipulate Cyrah.

"Right now, I just need my mom and dad, not Sable, the manager," Cyrah complained, nose turned up in disgust.

"I understand. It looks bad, and we can't let anything destroy what you've built." Sable rubbed her arms.

"Eric is the one trying to destroy it!" Cyrah yelled.

Sable looked shocked.

"Found it." Nicco walked over to me and held up a small black square tracker hidden in her makeup bag.

"He's getting bold," I admitted as I returned the device to Nicco.

He placed it in a clear plastic bag. "And dangerous."

"Maybe giving him what he wants will encourage him to out himself," I suggested, and all eyes watched me.

"What do you mean?" Nicco asked.

"Cyrah, in public," I said out of the corner of my mouth. I couldn't be too sure, but I thought Sable had a smirk on her face.

Nicco and I watched Cyrah and her parents continue talking. The information about Eric contacting her at the same time that Zander had possibly made contact at the lounge tonight put me on high alert. Earlier tonight, while Jasper had stayed with Cyrah on set, I'd been meeting the party planner for the governor's event.

"How many exits does it have?" I went over it in my head.

"Not sure, but that's her, right there." Nicco opened the door to the ballroom, where a woman stood with another couple and laughed.

The governor told us she would handle everything for the event, and I needed to coordinate my team for cover. The French president's spokesperson was showing up in his honor while he recovered, along with other high-profile politicians.

"Mrs. Ramirez." I stuck my hand out, and she turned to face me.

"Call me Octavia," she responded and smiled back.

"Octavia, we are here on behalf of the governor's security."

"Yes, he explained you'd come by the other day, but you had to cancel," she reminded us and thanked the couple before motioning for us to walk deeper into the ballroom. It held a large dance floor, stage, and about four exits I could see so far.

"Are you the man in charge?" Octavia questioned.

"Depends on who wants to know."

She grinned, licking her lips. "Are you single?"

I ignored her question. "Where is the governor coming from when he gives his speech?"

"The right corner and he will be sitting up front," Octavia answered.

"What about the media?" Nicco followed up.

"Every year, the governor puts on this event, and everybody wants to be seen. The media will for sure be here."

"I need every name and outlet to be screened," I told Nicco.

"That could take weeks." Octavia's brows bunched together.

"Then I suggest you cut it down to the top five because if anyone comes across our desk with a record, I will know about it." I looked around the room. It was completely bare at the moment, but she rambled on about the colors and decorations to represent his slogan and campaign.

"Nasir, did you hear me?" Cyrah questioned and snapped her fingers.

"No, what did you ask?" I shook out the thoughts of earlier today.

"I have an idea of how to bring out Eric." She leaned forward.

"How?"

"You be my boyfriend."

Crash!

A glass dropped out of Sable's hand, and she stomped

over to Cyrah. "Cyrah, are you crazy? That's the dumbest thing in the world."

"Let me handle this, please. I'm the one being stalked." Cyrah sat up on the couch and stood to stretch.

"Sable, maybe you should let Cyrah take the lead this time," her father agreed.

"No! How would it look if Cyrah stepped out with some guy after dating the governor's son? He's—I mean..." Sable stumbled with her words.

"Mrs. Brinkley, I'm not a fan of your daughter or you. But I never let my personal feelings mess with my job of protecting a client," I explained because she had nothing to worry about when it came to her daughter and me.

"I refuse." Sable glared at her daughter.

"Your opinion is not needed. This is my life, and someone is trying to kill me," Cyrah snapped, strolling out of the living room.

Sable started toward her, but I shifted around to block her. "Do you love your daughter, or is she just a dollar sign to you?"

Sable gasped, her mouth popping open and closed.

"Nas." Nicco called me by my nickname, and that meant I was going too hard on someone.

Her father looked ready to hit me with his fists clenched by his side.

"I apologize."

"Tell Cyrah we'll call her tomorrow." Sable angled around and left the house with her husband.

"Tonight was crazy, and we all said some things. Try to get some rest," Nicco said.

————

A week later, Cyrah and I went out to different events with me on her arm as her fake boyfriend. I despised the spotlight and tried to avoid it. At first, people tried to question me, but I left it up to Cyrah to answer those questions. We didn't argue as much as we had early on but had a mutual respect as we handled each other.

Right now, I was at the office while she was on set with Jasper and Nicco. I had the list of media companies attending the event and verified every detail before they were allowed approval.

Knock! Knock!

"Tell me you're going home at some point tonight." Amelia stood at the door of my office.

"What time is it?" I yawned, rubbed my eyes, sat up in my seat, and checked the time.

"Almost nine. Have you eaten?"

"A sandwich earlier."

Honestly, I had to give credit to Cyrah. The number of events she went to every day had me exhausted. The average person thinks they film a movie, and that's it, but she explained the events they do to promote, plus endorsements that some celebrities do to get a bigger brand that helps as an actor.

"Sounds like Aydin," Amelia joked, strolling to the chair and plopping down.

"Everything good with you two?" Even though Aydin was like my brother, I truly cared about Amelia as a little sister and would break his neck if he ever hurt her.

"He's good as usual. Same Aydin. But you're putting on a show with Cyrah," Amelia teased.

"A show?"

"Never did I expect you two would be able to be in the same room. Either you're acting, or some feelings have surfaced."

"Because someone is trying to kill her." I blew off her comment.

"Nicco could have managed her case," Amelia pointed out.

She was right, but the first night at the hospital, with our case being twisted in a web of lies with her ex-boyfriend, I'd started to feel sorry for her. "She can be a handful."

I logged into my email and responded to some urgent questions.

Amelia scooted down in the chair. "You like her." Her arm rested on the back of the chair.

"Amelia, don't start." I scratched my forehead, yawned once again, and covered my mouth.

"Not sure what you mean." She smiled.

"Trying to fix me up with somebody."

"When's the last time you went on a date?" Amelia demanded like a little sister often does in her brother's love life.

"Not having this conversation with you." Once the email box was clean, I took the stack of files from the outgoing box and filed them away in my cabinet.

"I think you're scared."

"I think you're delusional. This is business."

"I can see it in your eyes." Amelia followed me.

"Not everybody has the fairy tale like you and Aydin." I faced her and ruffled her hair.

She smacked my hand. "Come on, my relationship with Aydin didn't start that way."

I laughed. "True, but at least you could be in the same room as him."

"What's that supposed to mean?"

"Don't you have some work to do?" I came back to my desk as the door opened.

"No."

"She does, and I need to talk to him," Aydin interrupted.

Amelia rolled her eyes as he leaned down and pecked her on the lips. "All right, be like that, Nasir," she said as she sauntered out of my office.

I looked at Aydin. "What do you have?"

"Zander was spotted meeting with Eric."

"How do you know?"

"Offshore bank records show a deposit to Zander's account." Aydin passed a folder over.

I flipped it open to see large deposits in and out from an offshore account. "This could be evidence to bring to the DA."

"Governor might try to suppress it." One corner of his mouth twitched slightly.

"We can't let him know."

"Something else you should see." His voice held a bitter note. He pulled out a piece of paper from his pocket, and I took it from his hand.

"What's this?"

"The biggest problem." His eyes drew together in anger.

I flipped it open in confusion. "That's Eric." I pointed at him.

"Look at the woman with him," Aydin responded.

I lifted the photo because it was blurry. She wore glasses, but she was short and seemed older. "You have to be shitting me."

"Sable Brinkley," Aydin muttered.

"How old is this photo?" I flipped it over to see if it had a time and date stamp on the back.

"Not sure, but the team is looking into that and her bank records."

"Cyrah said it was an arrangement when she got with Eric," I said.

"Can't take the chance she's not behind the shooting," Aydin responded.

"Cyrah has a movie premiere tomorrow that I have to attend, and then the governor's event."

"Right now, just stick close to her, but don't spill anything until we know for sure her mother is legit," Aydin instructed.

I closed down my computer, deciding to head to her place tonight to give Jasper a break. Everybody took shifts on security detail at her home. Even though we hadn't caught Zander from the shootout, the tracker could have led him to her place.

Forty minutes later, I shut the door behind me, and Jasper left for the night. He told me Cyrah was on set today but wasn't in her usual mood. I dropped my bag near the front closet and went to the kitchen to find her standing in front of the window with a glass of wine.

"You're up late." We'd grown to respect each other, so I tried to be civil with my comment.

Cyrah turned. "Still wired from filming today."

I lifted the bottle of red wine that lay on the counter half-full. "Where's Brooks and the rest of the staff?" I scanned the kitchen.

"I gave them the rest of the night off." Cyrah raised the glass, sipped, then tugged on her ear.

Her schedule was pretty tight, and sleep was something she'd had very little of over the last few days. "Don't you have a premier tomorrow?"

"I do, but I'll be fine." She drank the rest of the glass and picked up the bottle to refill.

"You want to talk about your day?" This was an attempt to be a listening ear.

Her lips pressed in a thin line. "Why do you care?" she snarled at me, and the old Cyrah was back.

"Whether you like me or not, I'm on your side, Cyrah."

"Sorry. You're right. Just feels like someone is always watching me." Cyrah pulled out another bottle.

I took it out of her hand. "Have you eaten?" We had a little standoff.

"You sound like my mother."

I ignored her statement, opening the fridge for the left-over food her chef had prepared. "Eat something. I need you sharp for the governor's event."

Cyrah sat down on the stool and watched as I grabbed a plate and fork to fill with the pasta. I placed her plate in the microwave to warm it up.

"Do you think my mom loves me?" Cyrah blurted, catching me off guard.

Beep! Beep!

I removed her plate from the microwave and pushed it in front of her.

"Eat," I instructed, pulling the drawer open for a fork.

"Have some," she offered.

"I'm fine," I declined and watched her start to pick over her food.

"No, you are not letting me eat alone. Besides, as my boyfriend, you should want to eat with me on our date." Cyrah giggled drunkenly.

"The fake boyfriend card is only pulled in public."

"So you don't find me attractive?' She played with her food.

"Did I say you weren't attractive?" My left brow hiked up in surprise.

Cyrah and I stared at each other for a moment before she turned away.

"Enough about my depressing parents. Tell me about your family." Cyrah ate more of her food.

I stood against the counter with one ankle tucked underneath the other. "Grew up with my dad and Aunt Faye." I chuckled at the thought of Aunt Faye bossing my dad around.

"What made you join the Navy?" She pushed a little food into her mouth.

I rubbed my chin, sighing at the question. "I guess to prove something to myself and to have a real family I could count on."

Over time, the fellas and I had talked about the people we had back home, and I could hear the love some of the guys got with phone calls and letters from their parents and friends. My pops stayed in touch, along with my aunt, as much as they could.

"What happened to your mother?"

Her question stopped me for a second. I didn't know if I wanted to get that deep when we were just now getting on the same page. "She left us when I was young."

She frowned at my answer. "I can't imagine not having a mom as a kid."

I didn't feel guilty anymore. I knew it was on my mother as an adult. As the conversation grew more personal, I wondered how she felt about her mother. Because I hated to talk about mine. "My dad made sure I didn't want anything, plus my Aunt Faye is like a mom to me."

She nodded, flicking her hair out of her eyes. "So we both have some emotional baggage." She laughed.

I smirked. "Something like that, but I choose to push those emotions into my work while you…" I pointed at the glass of wine I'd removed.

"Ignore it with alcohol and become a bitch to all my friends," she finished.

"It's getting late."

"You're right. Time for bed so we can fake for the cameras another day." She giggled and stood up, carrying the plate to the sink and turning on the faucet to clean her dishes. A mask of reserve covered her face. "You can sleep in the guest room instead of the lumpy couch." She spoke from the doorway.

"Thanks."

Our eyes connected briefly, and her upper lip curved into a smile. Maybe we could co-exist and not hate each other before the end of this job.

I followed her out of the kitchen, lifted my bag off the ground, and headed for the stairs. I walked alongside her up to the guest room she pointed at, the third door across from her room. I slowly opened and then shut the door with a smirk.

"Cyrah Brinkley is something else," I whispered, admiring the king-size bed and TV mounted on the wall that looked around the same size as my father's. She had a few pictures of herself on the wall and a gray loveseat in the corner next to the closet.

"Home from home."

CHAPTER 8
Cyrah

"AMELIA, you know how much she drives me crazy."

Amelia had decided to take the day off work and hang out with me while I handled a few errands. After talking with Nasir, I'd had the urge to have a self-care moment and get away from everything and everyone. Amelia and I were on a spa treatment getting massages, then lunch and shopping.

"I remember all the times she cut you off from hanging out as a normal kid." Amelia turned to face me.

One woman worked on my shoulders, and the guy had Amelia face up, massaging her arms.

"Exactly, and people wonder why I keep a wall up. Even if I try to have a conversation with her, it's all about work and nothing about me as her daughter."

"Do you feel like a meal ticket?" Her lips were tense around the words.

"Sometimes, but I'm grateful for the sacrifice. I'm just venting." I spoke slowly and turned my head to face her.

Amelia reached over and grasped my hand. "No, you have the right to express your feelings."

"Nasir saw me drunk the other night, and I was embarrassed." I laughed, then moaned in relief when the masseuse worked on my feet.

"Oh, my God. What did you say?" Amelia turned her body and popped her elbow up under her chin.

After the massage, I sat on the table and tightened the towel around my body. "Made an ass out of myself. We talked about our childhood and his mom leaving him at an early age and growing up with his dad."

"Nasir welcomed me when I first came, way more than Aydin, and I think that's because he understands being abandoned or left out."

"How do you think it's going over with us pretending to be a couple?"

Amelia started to slide her feet into her shoes, and we headed to the bathroom to change. "Most social media is falling for you guys, but you know that can change in a second."

"Sable didn't like it at first, but I had to do something."

"Just be gentle with yourself and maybe have a conversation with her at some point on how you feel."

"You're right. Let's go have lunch." I stretched an arm around her shoulder.

"Do you have a dress for the party?" Amelia swung her head around to look at me.

"I do, and hopefully, it gets me on the best-dressed list."

Her eyes flashed to meet mine, and we slapped hands in the air.

Amelia chuckled and linked arms with me. "Still hard to believe you're a big-time actress, and I knew you as a little Cyrah from the neighborhood

"With my pigtails and glasses."

We burst into laughter.

"Do you like him?" Amelia climbed into the car after me, and the driver shut the door.

"Who?" I removed my makeup compact and reapplied

lipstick. Then I pulled some loose hair from my ponytail behind my ear.

Claude started to drive, and Amelia held out a packet of gum to share. "Nasir." Amusement gleaned in her eyes.

"It's a fake. Make-believe. Besides, he's not my type. Completely different from me." I poked her in the arm teasingly.

Amelia pursed her lips into a thin line.

"What is that look?' I twisted my body in my seat.

Claude stopped at the light and turned the music up a little. He knew I liked the classics from Luther and Marvin Gaye.

"Watching you lie to yourself." Amelia rolled her window down a little.

"I'm not lying." Perhaps there was a little truth to her words, but I'd never admit it. This fake boyfriend situation would wrap up when they caught the people threatening me. It was still hard to fathom that Eric was the one to put it in motion.

"Come on, Cyrah," she bantered, holding up her pinky finger in a challenge.

"Seriously, he's too broody and bossy." I swatted her finger down.

Amelia opened and closed her mouth, then snickered. "I see the diva is coming out."

"Not a diva. I just know what I like, and he's not into the lifestyle I lead."

"Has he said that?" she quizzed.

"Doesn't matter, Amelia. This is business. I need someone who will rock with me at all times, not someone who sees it as a burden," I murmured as the car pulled up to her office, I had a lunch planned, but depending on this conversation, it might turn into a late dinner.

Claude pulled alongside her office building.

"That's not fair, Cyrah."

"Claude, give us a few minutes."

"Sure, Miss Brinkley," Claude replied, keeping the car running.

"Sable corrupted your mind because Nasir is nothing but a sweet soul."

"Sable did one thing right. She showed me what type of husband I want." I slid my purse onto my arm.

"Who?" Amelia scratched her nose.

"Someone like my dad."

"Your dad lets your mom do anything and never takes up for you." Amelia started to open the door.

The point she'd just made was accurate. My mom ran all over my dad and never took my side. We could go back and forth all day and never agree on who was right in the conversation. Even growing up, plenty of times when a disagreement came about, our sisterhood would never become estranged.

I changed the subject. "What are you wearing, and is Aydin coming?"

"A simple dress with front top in lace and red, tight bodice, form-fitting."

"Good. Do you want my glam to do your hair and makeup?" I brushed a hand through her hair.

"We should just get ready together." She considered it the best option, and it saved time.

"Like old times." I felt rebellious tonight and would probably do a little flirting if I didn't have around-the-clock bodyguards. Maybe I could have a little space once they saw it was a relaxed event.

"Yep, let me go and grab some papers I forgot." Amelia started to get out of the car.

I looked out the window as Nasir and Aydin approached Amelia at the door. She must have said my name because they both looked back at me, and it felt like Nasir was staring right into my eyes.

"He's not my type," I mumbled under my breath to myself.

———

This was the ultimate test of how things would go for me moving forward. I breathed in and out slowly.

Nasir took my hand and helped me out of the car. Finally, after getting through traffic that had held us up for twenty minutes, we made it to the Premier event. After so many years, I should have been used to these types of settings, but they always made me nervous because of the large crowds. Everybody wanted my attention, either a photo or an autograph, plus other actors wanted to talk to do business.

Tonight's movie premier was extra special because we were raising money for charity, a good cause for literacy. Even though I could be known as a drama queen, I did give back to many causes. Governor Jones was expected to be the center of attention, but with us filming in Chicago and tax breaks, it looked good for us to mingle with political leaders and celebrities. After tonight, I hoped Eric would learn that I was never going back to him, and what we had was over.

"Cyrah! Cyrah! Are you planning a wedding?" a reporter asked as we walked the red carpet.

Nasir squeezed my hand, and I smiled at the flashing cameras. "All you guys think about is my love life. You do know I have a film coming out soon," I teased.

The reporter laughed. "We've seen the previews, and your fans are ready. But it's this guy right here who's stolen the spotlight." She pointed at Nasir, and he continued to look at his surroundings.

I planted my hand on his chest. He glanced down at me with a small smile, and I smirked. "He's the best, and we like to keep things private." The hand gesture had the crowd excited.

"Of course, you two look great together," a long-time reporter at most of the hottest premier events suggested.

"Thank you, Savannah," I said, slipping my hand into Nasir's.

"So it's always like this with reporters." Nasir led me through security.

I waved at Amelia and Aydin when I saw them approach. "Savannah's the biggest gossip, but most are not intrusive." Over my shoulder, I saw Savannah continue to stare at us.

"I could tell your voice seemed a little annoyed with her line of questioning." Nasir hugged Amelia.

"Aydin, you better watch out tonight. Your girl is looking like a million bucks," I joked.

He wrapped an arm around her waist and drew her in closer.

"We already argued in the car on the way here," Amelia said, rolling her eyes at him.

"The dress is painted on her." Aydin fussed and squeezed her tight.

I laughed at the two of them going back and forth.

"She looks good," I said, waving my hand for her to turn in a circle.

"Thank you, friend," Amelia answered with a curtsey.

"Are we all set for tonight?" Nasir looked at Aydin, and they both walked off together to whisper.

Amelia stood next to me with a glass of champagne in her hand. "I always wanted to come to these types of events."

Everyone looked like they didn't want to be here because it was an exercise in how well you could sell yourself.

"You don't miss much. It's all business, at the end of the day."

Large signs adorned the walls with my picture and the cast on them. Music played while everyone mixed and mingled.

"Cyrah, glad you made it on time. I have a few people that need to talk to you." Sable blocked Amelia from my view.

"Why can't we do the interviews afterward?" The words jolted nervously from my throat.

"Money never stops, Cyrah," Sable hissed.

She took my hand, and I excused myself from Amelia as Nasir glanced over his shoulder and started to approach us.

"Sable, slow down," I snapped as she pushed the hallway door open and continued down the hall.

"We don't have much time, so I lined up three interviews," she explained.

I snatched my hand away and rubbed my wrist when we approached an office door. "You should have told them to reschedule—" I stopped when the door opened, and Eric stood in front of me.

"Cyrah, thank you for coming," Eric said.

My brows dipped in anger, and nausea gripped my stomach. "What is going on?"

"Go and talk with Eric." Sable pushed me inside the room and started to shut the door.

"No! Sable, what is this?" My heartbeat quickened.

"Eric is here to apologize and make things right," Sable announced.

"Cyrah, we need to talk." Eric reached for my hand, but I slapped it away.

"There's nothing for us to talk about. You disgust me." No amount of apologies from him would make anything better.

"Cyrah, he made a mistake." Sable tried to reach for my shoulder in comfort, but I took a step back.

"You're my mother, and you're telling me I should take him back?" I argued in disbelief, shaking my head.

"Sable knows I love you." Eric stepped in front of me.

"Get out of my face." I shoved him back and stepped around him to leave. I turned to my mother and pointed a finger in her face. "Mothers are supposed to protect their children." *When did she feel so comfortable betraying me?* The only thing I wanted was to leave the room and find Nasir.

"Eric is harmless," Sable protested, clasping a hand around my wrist.

"Are you crazy? I need a drink. Leave me alone." I stomped off and returned to the party to find Nasir with Aydin and Nicco.

"Where did you go?" Nasir questioned solemnly.

"My mother tricked me." My cheeks burned as his eyes swept over me.

"What happened? You're shaking." Nasir rubbed my arms, helping me to sit down on the stool.

"She tried to get me to talk to Eric." I barely got it out before a tear fell.

Everybody got quiet.

"He's here?" Aydin probed, looking around the room.

All the men seemed ready to do damage, which could be the worst time for this to happen.

"Yes, and she wanted me to talk to him like it can all be forgiven."

"Amelia, stay with her," Nasir said. He started to walk off, but I grabbed his hand.

"Wait! Nas, please don't go." A sudden uneasiness crept up, and I needed Nasir close by. I wasn't sure where the sudden need for him not to get hurt came from.

"If he's here, that means Zander is near," Nasir reminded me.

"Nas is right," Amelia backed him up.

It made me paranoid at this point, and I started to look around the room.

"Nicco will stay with you. Aydin and I will go check it out." Nasir spoke.

"I'm going with you," I said, not wanting us to be split up.

"No, it's your premier. If you leave, people will get suspicious." Nasir caressed my cheek.

"Let them do their job, Cyrah." Amelia let me lean my head on her shoulder.

Nicco and a few other security details surrounded us. More people tried to approach. Minutes went by before the guys came back with disappointment on their faces.

"Did you find him?" I inquired.

"The room was empty."

As he said those words, the lights went out, plunging us into darkness.

"The lights! Oh, my God." A few people started to freak out and get upset.

"Cyrah!" I heard Nas's voice and reached out for him.

Pop! Pop!

"Arghhh!" I screamed as the lights came back on suddenly.

Crowds of people started to push and shove to get out. I was shoved back, lost between people trying to get to the exit. I glanced around the room to seek out Nasir and Amelia for help.

"Get out of the way!"

"Someone's shooting!"

"I've been shot!"

More and more people were yelling and crying from what had taken place. The doors opened, and police charged inside to clear the area. I tried to catch my breath and relax in the night air when I felt hands on my shoulder.

"Let me go!" I shouted, whipping around to see Nasir.

"It's me. Are you hurt?" Nasir ran a hand over my arms and back and down my stomach.

I leaned in and hugged him, tears spilling down my cheeks. "I thought it was him."

"He won't hurt you."

Panic spread through my body. "He's trying to kill me."

"Tell me what happened."

"Can we talk about this when we get home?" All my thoughts were jumbled together. Eric hated me enough to try and have me killed.

"The police will want a report from you."

"I know, but I'm so tired. This started as a good night, and now I'm wiped out."

"Cyrah, Nasir!" Amelia pushed through the crowd and wrapped her arms around me.

"Thank God you're safe." I removed one hand from Nasir and hugged Amelia.

"You, too. I can't believe something like this happened with so many high-profile people," Amelia remarked, her voice shaking with fury.

"It was the perfect setup," Nasir muttered.

I leaned into his chest, and he placed a hand on my hip.

"Where's your mother?" Aydin asked, biting out the question.

"Shit! My mom. I need to go back inside." I panicked.

"No, Nicco will stay with you, and I'll go back and check for her."

"Nas, I don't want to be alone," I blurted.

"Okay, I'll get Nicco to go check," Nasir answered.

"Thanks. I just feel safer with you near."

Nasir and I became closer after the movie premier shooting. The career I'd planned out for myself was beginning to look a little fickle. Too much surrounded me wherever I went, and I felt the weight of the target on my back.

Nasir continued to work and sleep in the guest room to keep my worries at bay. Today, I had plans to treat him to breakfast, and we'd talk. Later, he was supposed to have dinner with his father and aunt. He'd invited me to go, and at first, I declined because it felt too intimate.

"Morning. I hope you're hungry." I flipped the pancake and tossed a few pieces of bacon on the plate. Brooks had been given the day off, and I planned on finally telling Nasir everything about Eric. Governor Jones had never responded about the whereabouts of his son, and I feared he may have tipped him off and gotten him out of the country.

"You cook," Nasir teased, sitting down on the stool.

I was distracted by him only wearing a pair of sweatpants and no shirt. His six-pack and broad shoulders would have any girl gawping.

I cleared my throat. "Funny, but I can cook a little something." A thin smile edged my lips.

"Surprised Brooks let you in his kitchen," Nasir joked, pouring coffee into his cup.

"Well, it wasn't easy, but I needed to talk to you alone." Now was the worst time for me to feel nervous with Nasir.

He stared at me and sipped his coffee as he leaned against the counter. "Go ahead."

I'd started to believe that was his favorite spot in my house because you could see who was coming in front and on the side from the window.

I fidgeted with my hands and released a deep breath. "It's about my relationship with Eric." I planted my hands on my back and stood in front of him.

"What about it?"

"It was more a business arrangement—well, it started that way. Our parents thought we could help each other."

"Like an arranged marriage." His lips curled into a scowl.

"Not completely. We dated to boost his political campaign and my career."

"Your mother is cold." He whistled, turning to grab the coffee pot and filling his cup.

"She can be, but I agreed to go along with it because I wanted to get far in my career."

"Your talent will get you there." Nasir was adamant.

"Not that simple, Nasir."

"You loved him?" He inclined his head forward. Something in his tone suggested he would be pissed if I said yes.

"Never in love, but I cared for him after a while. But then he cheated and became very controlling."

"Did he hurt you?" A vein throbbed on his forehead.

"Not physically, but he always needed to be in control of how I acted as his woman. He told me if he took on a big political move, I would need to quit my career."

"That's when you broke up?" Nasir started to piece things together.

"Partially, but he cheated as usual, and I wanted out."

"How did your parents handle the breakup?"

"Sable hated it and wanted me to stick around. The opportunities were too big to lose."

"Damn." Nasir took a deep breath.

"Exactly. No matter what, it's about getting to the next level with her." My mouth pulled to one side in a grimace.

"Has a conversation happened with your mom?"

"No. Amelia thinks I should sit down and tell her how I feel, but I know deep down she cares."

"I can only tell you what I know, and from the outside looking in, your life is constant chaos, Cyrah. If we hadn't crossed paths that night, you would be dead right now."

His words made me feel guilt and sorrow. I'd been too naïve about the situation. Too often, I'd tried to protect Eric, and it was biting me in the ass. He was trying to kill me because I didn't want to be with him anymore.

"He's never going to stop, is he?" I started to feel hopeless.

"Afraid not, and I need to get the police report from the other night."

I gave him a puzzled look. "How did a gun get inside?"

"Probably paid someone off."

"Should I stay home for the rest of my life?"

He grinned. "You wouldn't be Cyrah Brinkley if you let people control your life."

I laughed at his statement. "Tell me about this dinner at your father's house tonight." I reached for the syrup and poured a small amount, using the knife to cut my pancake into small pieces.

"A casual Thursday night dinner we have weekly. Don't come as Cyrah the superstar, or my Aunt Faye will curse you out."

"See, maybe I should stay home." My throat went dry.

He laughed at my joke and reached over to cover my palm. The few moments of laughter made me feel better about the next steps I was going to take with my career. The studio had canceled the LA project, so I was stuck in Chicago with no upcoming gigs until everything cooled down and they found the person trying to kill me.

"Seriously, with everything that's happened, do you need to talk to someone?" Nasir put the cup down and gripped my left hand in comfort.

I focused on my plate of food. "At some point, I thought she would see me as her daughter and not a meal ticket." I was growing frustrated with the many times Sable had disappointed me.

"You don't call her mom?"

I wiped the excess syrup off my hands. "A few times growing up, I called her mom, but she preferred Sable. After a while, I got used to doing it that way."

"What are the odds we both have issues from our parents?" Nasir asked, popping a piece of bacon in his mouth.

"Has your mom tried to contact you at all? I mean, now that you're grown?"

He shook his head. "No, and I don't need her at this point. Aunt Faye is the woman I see as my mother."

"Excited to meet this Aunt Faye." A nervous chill reached the bottom of my spine when he brought her up.

"She's a trip but extremely loyal." The tone of his voice showed she was important to him. "Thanks for breakfast. I need to get some work done before we head out for dinner tonight."

Nasir stood, took his empty plate to the sink, and rinsed it. I stared at his back as he left with foolish thoughts of what it would be like to be in his arms beyond bodyguard and client.

CHAPTER 9
Nasir

I NEVER THOUGHT Cyrah and I would sit down together and have a real conversation as human beings without constantly bickering with each other. We'd come a long way, with Cyrah letting down her guard and talking about the issues with her mother and me confiding about growing up without mine. We realized that we had something in common, despite being polar opposites. She was Hollywood: she loved the spotlight and being in front of the camera. Partying and socializing as an extrovert was what drove her. On the other hand, I loved to be at home. I was introverted and didn't care about the amount of money someone had or need people to cater to my every need.

Cyrah allowed me to work in her office, and after the movie premiere, she was more afraid to be seen in public. She'd grown attached to me and wanted me with her twenty-four seven until we caught Eric and the hired gun. That moment the lights went out was an out-of-body experience. Not knowing where she was or if someone had touched her and I couldn't protect her.

It took me back to my time at war and seeing the eyes of the people who were helpless and needed someone to make a difference, to make things better. The fear when I first got into dangerous missions quickly faded because I knew my men had my back and I had theirs. For life, we'd be brothers, and worked to make sure we protected the innocent.

Ring! Ring!

I lifted my cell phone to answer, flipping through the rest of the report.

"I hear you're looking for me." A hint of sarcasm eased into his voice.

My brows lifted in surprise. "Who am I speaking with?"

"She's not yours." Jealousy was the first thing I picked up on, and I knew who was calling me.

"Eric Jones." Something told me to stay calm and not let him hear that I was upset. Narcissists like him fed off being in control; that was how they tried to manipulate.

"If you want to see another day, you'll leave her alone," Eric said in an abrasive tone.

"Cyrah is my girlfriend." That statement would put him on edge.

Eric chuckled devilishly through the phone. "A woman like Cyrah doesn't hang with your kind. She needs a man of my stature," he mocked.

"The stature of a guy who has to pay to get a girlfriend," I taunted.

The line went silent. "Cyrah and I will be married soon, and then I'm going to make sure you're forgotten." His voice cracked.

"Let me get this straight. You think Cyrah will take you back after trying to kill her multiple times," I said in an amused voice.

"She will understand. I had to do something for her to take me seriously," Eric responded.

"You do realize you're sick. Cyrah will never be with you."

"Tell that to Sable," Eric replied.

"What is that supposed to mean?" Aydin had already informed me about Sable and the photos, but the more information he spilled, the better.

"Sable knows what is good for Cyrah, and being with me will take her beyond her wildest dreams."

"Hey, Nas, what kind of food is Faye cooking tonight?" Cyrah barged into her office.

"Is that my future wife? Tell her I said hi." Eric laughed and hung up.

I slammed my hand down on the desk. "Fuck!"

"If you don't want me to go, just say." Cyrah stood at the side of the desk with a scowl on her face.

I blew out a breath and dropped the phone on the desk.

"That was Eric." I leaned back in the chair, folded my hands together up to my face, and stared forward in thought.

"Eric Jones, my ex?" She could see I was angry.

"Yeah." I ran a hand down my face.

"How did he get your number?"

"Not sure, but he's just crazy, as you mentioned." I finally focused intently on her.

———

Aunt Faye stirred the pot of greens on the stove and slapped my hands when I tried to scoop up some baked beans before the food was ready. Cyrah stood next to her at the stove and laughed when she cursed me out. Seeing her dressed in casual jeans, a turtleneck, and her hair wrapped in a low bun with light makeup showed she wanted to present herself to my family as Cyrah Brinkley of Chicago and not the Hollywood actress.

"Nasir, stay out of this kitchen, boy," Aunt Faye fussed, reaching for the black pepper for the sauce. She was making her famous ribs, baked potato, beans, rice, and cornbread, plus Kelis was visiting from college.

"Aunt Faye, I thought I was the favorite."

"Not when it comes to sneaking out of pots," Aunt Faye argued.

Kelis stuck her tongue out at me. "Tell him, Momma. As the girl in the family and youngest, I get first dibs," she taunted and shoved me in the back.

"Youngest, but you got suspended from school in tenth grade, and I covered for you."

She gasped, and Cyrah shook her head at me.

"Kelis! You got suspended from school?" Aunt Faye turned toward Kelis with a deep frown on her face.

"Momma, he's lying. It was him who got suspended." Kelis tried to pin it on me.

I walked over to Aunt Faye, stretched my arm around her shoulder, and teased Kelis from behind with a roll of my eyes. "Aunt Faye knows I would never lie to her."

Aunt Faye cocked her head to the side. "Child, lie to somebody who doesn't know you. Anyway, Cyrah, you are more than welcome to come here anytime, even without my nephew."

"How are you going to invite her to my father's house without me?"

Aunt Faye pushed the bowl of beans and cornbread into my hand. "Easy. I run this house because your father has my name on the deed."

The women laughed at me.

"Take that to the table, boy," Aunt Faye commanded.

"Thank you for the invitation, Miss Faye." Cyrah shuffled in her seat.

"Call me Aunt Faye or Faye, sweetie," she replied, lifting the tray of ribs and coming to the dining room table.

"Cyrah, what's it like to work on movies?" Kelis asked.

"Fun and sometimes exhausting," Cyrah responded, taking a scoop of rice on her plate.

"Have you ever met Eddie Murphy?" Dad asked as he drank his beer. Eddie Murphy was one of his favorite movie stars.

"I know this is cliché, but the cameras don't do you justice. You're gorgeous, girl," Kelis complimented.

Cyrah thanked her. "Kelis, you beat me in the looks department. And, no, I haven't met him, sir." She answered my dad's question.

I playfully ruffled Kelis' hair, and she shoved me on the shoulder. She looked at Cyrah. "How long have you and my cousin been dating?"

Cyrah and I went silent.

"Kelis," Aunt Faye screeched, pointing her fork in her direction.

Cyrah nervously shifted in her seat.

"Um…huh." Kelis sank down in her seat.

"Tell the truth." Aunt Faye gave Cyrah a look.

"What are you talking about, old woman?" I demanded.

"You and Cyrah aren't really a couple." Aunt Faye's lips formed into a satisfied smile that she might have caught on to our fake relationship.

"How do you know?" Cyrah inquired.

"Well, in the first videos and photos, you two looked distant, but from seeing it up close, I can tell you like my nephew, and he cares for you," Aunt Faye commented.

Cyrah kept her eyes low. My aunt was right that Cyrah and I couldn't stand each other in the beginning, but not as we grew closer and spent more time together. Her life started to make more sense to me. She put up a wall to keep people out, to keep her emotions hidden as she lived a life in front of the camera.

"Faye, leave the boy alone. You are always in somebody's love life," Dad preached, bringing a piece of cornbread to his mouth, then wiping his hands with the napkin.

"Nas knows as his mother figure. I have to check out any woman he brings home to meet me. No offense to Cyrah, but I was worried when I first saw you two together."

"None taken, and we aren't together," Cyrah replied.

"What do you mean?" Kelis queried.

"It's fake," I admitted and popped open the beer bottle.

"Fake to the world, not to me," Aunt Faye responded, smirking.

"He's only my bodyguard," Cyrah blurted, her eyes scanning from Faye to my dad.

"You two can keep lying, but Aunt Faye sees the truth," Dad muttered.

"I know that's not just lemonade, probably a little vodka or something," I joked to cut the tension in the room. Cyrah and I faked the entire relationship for the cameras, but nothing would come of it, and I prided myself on not involving myself with a client.

"As the woman who changed your diapers, I can drink what I want." Aunt Faye checked me like always, and we laughed.

———

The family dinner went by fast, and almost a week later, Aunt Faye did nothing but ask when Cyrah was coming over again. I'm not sure what she did to my family, but even my father liked her, and Kelis got invited to come on set when she filmed again. Seemed like I became the favorite in the family with Cyrah on my arm.

Tonight, I had Cyrah pick the fanciest restaurant where all the celebrities went for photographers, and we got a table at Craig's in West Hollywood. Our waitress finished pouring our wine and left us alone in the back corner of the booth. This was the first time I'd been here, and it was a place that had been here for many years. It reminded me of classic Hollywood, with an intimate setting for customers.

"Thanks for dinner. I know it's all pretend, but it's nice to get out for a change," Cyrah muttered.

"I thought a dinner out of the house would make up for my family." I chuckled.

"Your family is great." Cyrah cupped her hand under her chin and leaned on the table with her elbow.

I faked a roll of my eyes. She giggled, and I smiled at her being relaxed in front of me. Then I placed a finger to my lips and acted like we should be quiet. "Shush. Don't let my cousin and aunt hear you say how much you like them."

A couple slowly walked over to our table. The woman seemed like she was about to pass out at seeing Cyrah. "I'm so sorry. Is it possible to get a picture with you?" she pleaded excitedly.

"Do you mind?" Cyrah inquired, and I motioned for her to go ahead.

"She's a huge fan," her husband said.

The wife leaned down, and Cyrah placed her arm around her and smiled. The waitress stood to the side with our food, and he took the picture. I waited for him to finish, and Cyrah signed a napkin. The couple thanked her.

"You ordered the ribolita, tortellini with ravioli, and arancini for you, ma'am," the waitress announced. We both thanked her and started to dig into our food.

"Maybe I should have ordered what you got." Cyrah pointed at my plate.

"Are you saying you're one of those?" I put my fingers in air quotes.

"One of what?"

"Hate what you order and then eat off the other person's plate." I laughed.

She kissed her teeth and picked up her fork. I grabbed the glass of water. Unlike at my folks' house, I didn't want to be caught under the influence when Eric tried to make a move.

"Can you be honest with me?" Cyrah slid the fork into her mouth.

The guys would tell me not to give too much away on the case, especially with how controlling her mother was toward her. "Depends."

"Not asking for everything, just what happened at the movie premier to Eric calling you." She continued to eat.

"He told me to leave you alone, that you belong to him."

"What did you say?" Cyrah laid a hand to her lips.

"Does it matter?" A frown creased my forehead.

We had a stare-off.

"It matters because it's my life." Cyrah shook her head fiercely.

"Trust me, he's not going to hurt you."

She dropped her fork on her plate. "And the guy he hired?"

"We have some leads."

"Sounds like you have no clue." She slowly turned her head and rolled her eyes.

Because I needed Cyrah to trust we would find Eric and Zander, I would fill her in on some more details so she could at least be equipped if something else came about.

"Did you see yourself marrying Eric?"

That made her whip her face around to me. "Where did that question come from?" Her mouth compressed into a hard line.

There was truth in my comment. "I want us to be honest."

"Eric proposed, but like I said, he cheated so much, and I wasn't going to be a fool for anybody." The words leaped out of her mouth.

"What about your relationship with his father?"

"The governor is all about perception with the public. Everybody in a position of power is like that."

"The person he hired that night was a former military man, very good at his job. I'm not sure how Eric found him."

"Are you saying you think the governor is involved somehow?" She stretched her arms out.

"Never rule it out," I concluded.

"So, what would that mean?" She stopped talking like a lightbulb went off in her head and leaned back against the chair.

"What are you thinking?"

She glanced around the restaurant, leaned forward, and whispered, "My mother."

I hated to confirm anything regarding her mother. I had my own issues from growing up without my mom, so I had no relationship to compare, but even though Sable was not mother of the year, Cyrah still loved her.

"Do you want to go home?"

"I need to see what information you have." Cyrah stroked her hair.

"Cyrah." My brows scrunched up.

"Nasir, you're sitting here, and my mother could be involved."

"Never said she was involved, but it's suspicious with her trying to get you to talk to Eric."

"The movie premier was an attempt for her to get us back together and nothing more. I can't believe she would be helping to get me killed." Her face wrinkled in disgust.

"Those words never came from me."

Something flashed in her eyes. "Take me to your office," she responded, looking at me intently.

"Why?"

Cyrah threw her napkin down on the table, picked up her purse, and stood up from the booth. "Trust, remember," she answered.

I reached in my pocket, removed my wallet, and left enough for a tip. Then I took Cyrah's hand. We walked out of the restaurant, and I passed my ticket to the valet. He arrived a few seconds later with my car. I held the door open for Cyrah and hurried to the driver's side.

"Cyrah, it's late. Maybe we should talk about everything tomorrow." I sped out into traffic.

She removed her phone and started to dial someone.

"Who are you calling?" I glanced from the road to her.

"Sable."

I snatched the phone out of her hand and hung up.

"Nasir!" she screamed.

I swerved to avoid another car. "Shit! You okay?" I cupped her shoulder, lifting her chin to face me.

Cyrah held her hand to her chest to control her breathing.

I hit the right turn signal, pulled off to the side of the road, put the car in park, unhooked my seatbelt, and cupped her chin to turn her toward me.

"Just relax and take a deep breath." To keep her trust, I needed to get her to relax.

She withdrew from me. "Take me home," Cyrah demanded, her face livid.

"Until we know all the details, Sable can't know anything."

Cyrah wiped a tear that spilled down her cheek. "Does the information you have include anything on my mother?"

I threw my head back against the seat. "A photo of her

with him." No matter what, she wanted the truth, and I couldn't hold off any longer.

"Is it recent?"

"Not sure." I pressed my hand on the steering wheel.

Cyrah shook her head. "Then you don't know for sure."

"Cyrah—"

"Give me some kind of hope, Nas," Cyrah muttered and looked up with sadness in her eyes.

"I'm taking you home." I reached behind me to secure my seatbelt, started the car, got back on the road, and headed for her place.

CHAPTER 10

Cyrah

IT WAS wishful thinking on my part that someone could love me beyond what I could do for them or spoil them with the perks of Hollywood. My entire life was planned out to become the famous Cyrah Brinkley, the girl from the local neighborhood with charm and charisma. After what happened at the governor's last night, I'd been a fool for too long. I'd allowed many people to speak for me and control how I should be. It was why I pushed Nasir whenever he challenged me because, to him, I was just Cyrah. Our brief time together had stirred up so many emotions, and I wasn't sure I could ever go back to what I used to be.

I inhaled the night air and blinked back the tears attempting to escape over the situation that had destroyed my entire world.

"Cyrah, listen." He fixed his eyes on me.

"Go away, Nasir." My voice trembled.

"I will when I know you're okay." He placed his hand on my back.

I closed my eyes and released a deep breath. For him to see me in my raw emotions meant I cared what he thought of me. I hated how vulnerable I was, not the bold, in-your-face Cyrah. I turned around and let him see the tears that continued to flow.

"You win." I forced a demure smile.

His face showed confusion. "What did I win?" He moved in to close the space between us, and my chest tightened and heaved up and down.

"You were right. I'm not worth the hassle. My family is a lie, along with my career. It's probably best you leave now."

I took another sip of the vodka and lime before Nasir snatched it out of my hand, then walked back into the house.

"Give that back!" I shouted. I marched behind him into the kitchen.

He poured it down the drain. "You're drunk." He pointed at me angrily.

"No, I'm not. It was the first glass." I waved him off.

"Drink some water." He opened the fridge and took out a bottle of water.

"My life is in shambles, and you want me to drink water."

"I want you to act like a woman who doesn't take crap from anyone and fight back!" he shouted.

I jumped back in surprise. "Done fighting." Even with him throwing one glass out, I could refill from the bottle I had in the fridge.

"So they win," Nasir remarked, not a vestige of humor on his face.

"Nasir." I whispered his name.

He came around the island and hugged me. I cried for all the times I'd listened to my mom tell me she was taking care of me. All the times she'd smiled in my face when a deal closed, and I saw my name in lights on the billboard.

"She never loved me." I pulled back and wiped my face.

"Your mother loves you, deep down," Nasir replied.

"Thank you for saving me." I finally took a moment to study Nasir's features up close and saw the soft warmth in his eyes.

I leaned forward and pressed my lips against his. He pulled me in closer and ran one hand up my back to my neck and the other down to my butt cheek. I groaned into his mouth. I snaked my tongue in and out, and he angled us around with my back to the counter and sucked on my bottom lip.

Nasir released his hold on me and ran his eyes over my body. "What are we doing?"

"I want this for real."

"I'm not like the past men you've dated, Cyrah."

"Just don't hurt me, Nas." Our hands intertwined.

"If I hurt you, it only hurts me. That would never happen intentionally."

He gripped me around the waist, set me on the counter, and leaned down to suck on my neck. My head fell back, and I wrapped my legs around his waist. The straps of my nightgown fell, and Nasir tweaked my nipples.

"Want to feel you all night long, Nas." I inclined my head back.

"When I first saw you in the gown that night, I dreamed about snatching it off and tasting you as you screamed my name," Nasir muttered.

I closed my eyes as his hands reached between my legs and pulled my panties down to my ankles. I kicked them out of the way.

"Take me upstairs." I waited breathlessly for his response.

"Takes too long. I want to taste you right now." He dropped to his knees and kissed my thigh, pushing my left leg over his shoulder. He held onto the counter as if he had gone to another place while my juices poured down my thighs.

"Ummm," I moaned. My chest rose, then fell, and my stomach dropped.

His tongue slipped in and out, then he grabbed my leg tightly and pulled me off the counter as he stood.

"Nas! Put me down." I not only felt lightheaded, but my stomach held butterflies.

He moaned and shifted me flat on my back to the floor, removing my gown, and hovering over me with lust-filled eyes. "I want you for real. No more fake bullshit."

All I could do was nod in agreement. There was no more pretend with us. "Kiss me." I helped to remove his shirt and unbuckle his pants.

He ran a hand over my lips. My head fell back, and I opened my legs in anticipation. His stiff dick poked my entrance and made me shiver in anticipation. I clung to his broad shoulders as he slid inside me.

"So fucking sexy." Nas groaned.

He lowered his head in the crook of my neck, extending his hands to capture mine and moving them above my head as he rocked back slowly.

"Stop torturing me," I whispered, trying to remove my hands from his tight grip.

Finally, he released his hold, and I slid my hand around his back. I arched beneath him and felt him grow even harder when I squeezed my thighs around his waist. Nas sat up and watched himself move in and out of me. He knew what he was doing, and even with me being a year celibate, I hadn't forgotten how to please a man.

"You okay?" Nasir asked as he picked up my leg and kissed my inner thigh.

"Ooooh..." I cooed, trying to thrust back.

He chuckled. "Finally got you quiet...huh?"

I wouldn't let him win this round, so I clamped down on his dick.

"Fuck! Cyrah, stop that shit." He reached out and tugged on my hair.

I licked my lips and reached up to grip his face as he planted his hands on my hips and pulled out of me fast.

"Nas!" I snapped as he flipped me around to get on my knees and eased back inside in a quick thrust.

"You are not running this, Miss Brinkley." Nasir slapped me on the ass and grabbed a handful of my hair.

I slammed my hand on the floor as his pelvis hit my ass.

"Who's in charge, Cyrah?" His deep voice spoke in my ear.

"You are!" I screamed and felt my heart expand with so much passion and pain from everything I'd been through over the years up to meeting him. For him to see the real me and not run away despite the number of times I'd pushed back was a blessing.

"Are you ready to come, baby?" Nasir whispered in my ear.

"Yes." I felt my stomach flutter and tears languish down my cheeks.

He was so intimate and patient. He lifted my back to his chest, slowed his strokes, and played with my clit, turning my head to kiss me on the lips until I came.

"You don't have to be afraid of me," he whispered in my ear.

The dam between my legs erupted, and I covered his palm as I convulsed in his hold. He came right behind me and held me tight against him. I finally caught my breath, tilted my head to one side, and studied the expression on his face.

———

The night before replayed in my head, and I groaned at the sudden headache that wouldn't leave me alone. Before I could get up and take care of the migraine, a large arm was blocking me from getting out of bed. I shifted around to see Nasir lightly snoring, completely naked under the covers with his dick against my ass. I slowly tried to move his arm, and he pulled me in closer and kissed the back of my neck.

"Morning." His voice was groggy as he spoke.

"Morning." I stared at his handsome features.

He slowly popped both eyes open. "Trying to sneak out on me?" he asked groggily.

"I was going to brush my teeth and take care of this migraine." I eased my hand under the covers to rub against his chest.

"What do you have to do today?" He touched my face, gently caressing my cheek.

"Figure out why my mom lied to me and then make some arrangements to get a new manager."

"Sorry. I had no choice but to tell you."

"Not your fault." I caressed his cheek.

"Even though we started out as two ranging bulls, I like this new path." Nasir appraised my naked figure under the covers.

"Do you?" I grinned, rubbing his cheek.

Knock! Knock!

"Ugh, I just want to be left alone." I slid my bottom lip between my teeth.

"Go take care of that breath and I'll grab the door." He tossed the covers back on the bed.

Afraid he would leave and not come back, I grabbed his arm. "You aren't leaving, are you?"

"No, just to answer the door and grab some coffee for us." Nasir smirked, then leaned over the bed and kissed me on the forehead.

I relaxed, climbed out on the other side of the bed, picked up the nightgown, and rushed into the bathroom.

"Uh, is Cyrah available?" I heard Mikka's familiar voice.

I turned the shower on and stuck my head out of the bathroom with the toothbrush in my mouth.

"She's in the shower." I overheard Nasir talking.

A few seconds later, the door opened, and he strolled over behind me, pulling me against his chest. He kissed the back of my ear. "Mikka wants to know if you're available to do a few shout-outs before you go on set today."

I spat out the toothpaste, washed my mouth, and turned to face him. "What do you have planned today?" The words sprang off my lips of their own accord.

He massaged my shoulder and pressed his lips to it. "See the governor and try to get a location for his son."

For a moment, we stared at each other in the mirror.

"Eric's probably off to some foreign country." Nasir grabbed the other toothbrush. I handed him the toothpaste, and a few seconds later, he rinsed out his mouth. "He has a fiancée, and I doubt she wants to up and move."

"She's a paid fiancée. Nothing in that family is real." I angled around to face him.

"So you doubt she loves him." Nasir's teeth glinted in a snarky smile.

"She loves the money. Eric wants me back only because I moved on. Hates losing."

Nasir looked deep in thought. "His father must have cut him off, and that's why he's trying to take him down."

"Probably, but I just want to be here in your arms while I still can."

"I promise to wrap up quickly. Jasper is downstairs with Mikka."

"Okay, but can you shower with me first?" I motioned with my finger for him to follow, slid the door open, and climbed inside.

Nasir removed his sweats, and I bit my bottom lip at his long, thick pole standing at attention.

"Only one round, Miss Brinkley."

He lifted me against the corner of the wall. As the water spray drizzled down, I removed the head of the shower and positioned it over my head to wet my hair and then over him. When he took it out of my hand and lowered it along my pussy, he circled his thumb against my wetness, and my mouth opened in awe.

"Right there...uh, huh," I cooed and started to hump against his finger.

"You look sexy as fuck." His right hand lowered to my ass, then Nasir slipped his long, fat dick inside me and took my breath away.

"Nassssiiiirrr!" I moaned.

The care he took and his strokes to know how to make me come was magical. It was like I'd never had sex before him with the way he touched me, and I felt my juices seep out of me. Our sex noises sounded so good I wanted to record them and have them with me forever as a reminder before it all ended. The way my pussy grew uncontrollably wet knocked my breath away.

"Mmmmm...like when you let go with me," Nasir complimented me.

He bent his head and sucked on my nipple as his strokes grew faster, then pulled out and released on the floor.

Forty minutes later, I was dressed and downstairs with Mikka to discuss my schedule, sitting in my office with drinks while my last film played on the TV screen.

"Smiling with a glow." It was a compliment that Mikka gave me.

"Besides Amelia, you're the only person I will let get on my nerves. I always smile."

"Sure you do." Mikka mocked me, both cheeks rising in a wide smile.

"Ugh, I might need a new assistant."

Mikka laughed. "Let's talk about the elephant in the room."

I picked up the cup, sipped on the ginger ale, and scrolled on social media. Brooks had made breakfast, but we'd missed it because of our shower, and now Nasir was on his way to work. We planned on having lunch or dinner together.

"The fact that I saw Nasir in your bedroom this morning is cause for a conversation."

"Fine, Mikka, but I'm having this conversation only once."

Mikka sat up promptly and clasped her hands together, ready for my answer.

"We had dinner together, and then we talked."

"And—" Mikka wagged her hand for me to keep talking.

"I was upset, and he calmed me down." My voice was laced with irritation.

"So you ended up on your back with his dick in you because you were upset," Mikka suggested.

"Why did I hire you again?"

"Come on, Cyrah. The man is gorgeous. You don't need to tell me all the details."

"I wasn't planning to. He told me something about Eric and my mother, and I had a drink or two."

"One thing led to another."

"I wasn't drunk, just betrayed and needed to release some feelings."

"Well, that's the best way to get feelings out," Mikka joked.

"All right, get back to work and run down my schedule."

"Yes, Miss Brinkley," Mikka teased.

"Can't stand you."

"I know. I love you, though. Sable has a few foreign endorsements for you to look into for next week."

"Scrap them. If you can't, send the information to my lawyer to ensure the contracts are fair but leave Sable out of any communications."

Mikka had a confused look on her face. "Is there something I should know about?"

"Going forward, anything with my career needs to come to me first. If Sable tries to set something up, confirm with me."

"Okay, but does Sable know this?"

"She will in time. At some point, you'll find out, but Sable has done a few shady things behind my back."

Surprise lifted Mikka's brows. "Sable's your mom, Cyrah."

"Which makes me cringe from what I've heard about her." I flung my head back and groaned in frustration.

"From the look on your face, it must be bad."

Knock! Knock!

Nasir stood at the door, and I waved him inside.

"Heading into work?" I asked.

"Yes, but I'm more concerned with you." He caressed my cheek.

"Huh."

He bent down and rubbed my thigh. "What's wrong?" His eyes narrowed as he searched my face.

"How do you know something is wrong?" I studied him and lifted our hands together.

He tilted my chin down to stare into his eyes. "Because the smile is not there from earlier." Nasir tapped my nose.

I pecked his lips twice, then wiped the excess lipstick off. "You're right, but I'll be fine. Mikka knows I have a few things to handle with Sable."

Nasir stood up, lifted my hand, and kissed my palm. "Jasper is here, and I'll be back later," he announced and walked out.

"I wouldn't have to fake being his girlfriend," Mikka mumbled under her breath.

I cocked my head and pointed my finger. "Eyes over here—besides, it was a one-time thing," I lied to myself.

If Nasir wanted to pursue a relationship with me, I would do so without hesitation. I hoped he could be part of my world as much as I needed to be part of his.

CHAPTER 11
Nasir

POP! Pop!

"He's on the run."

I ran through the house with my gun drawn to catch up to Zander, but he escaped. Nicco had sent me a text on my way to the office and told me to meet at this location because of a tip that Zander had been spotted here a few nights ago. Most of the team was back at the office except for Nicco, Aydin, and Vaughn.

I saw Aydin climb the fence, reached it in time, and went over. Vaughn stayed behind as the neighbors called the police. Zander had a five-minute head start on us but slipped and ran into a bunch of kids playing outside. I crossed through the same backyard, down the steps, and up the alley as Aydin closed in on him. Zander stood, reached for his gun, and sent more shots toward us.

Pop! Pop! Pop!

"Give it up!" I shouted, ducking behind the wall of the main street.

Aydin went behind a car. It wasn't too crowded with traffic, but a few people were out and started to scream and run.

"Not a chance," Zander yelled.

"Argh! Help me!" a woman screamed.

I saw Zander was holding a woman in front of him at gunpoint.

"Shit." I wiped the sweat off my forehead. Zander was unpredictable, and we wouldn't take him alive unless we could offer him a way out.

I glanced at Aydin, and he motioned to cover him. I shook my head no. If something happened to him, Amelia would never forgive me.

"What do you want?" I came around the back wall and held my hands up in surrender.

Zander smirked. "Where's the girl?"

"Let her go." My eyes ducked to the left at Aydin as he slowly crawled to the front side of the car to get a better shot at Zander.

"What do I get in return?"

"Your life," I hissed.

He laughed and gripped her around the neck.

"Agh!" she screamed when he put her in a headlock.

Pop! Pop! Pop!

The girl dropped to the ground. Zander stumbled backward when the bullets went through his chest, and I sent a shot into his stomach, then legs.

Aydin rushed over and pulled the girl behind him, kicking the gun out of the way. I jogged toward them and held my gun up as Zander's breath slowed down. Blood leaked out of his mouth, and his eyes stared up at me.

"Who paid you?" I barked as he cradled his chest.

He smirked, then choked on his cough.

"Where is Eric?" Aydin bent down close to Zander.

"Fuuuccckkk youuu." Zander's eyes closed, and his hand fell to the side as he took his last breath.

I bent down to check his pulse. Police sirens and an ambulance arrived shortly afterward, and Aydin helped the young woman get checked out. Police roped off the area and pulled me to the side for questioning.

"She's a little freaked out, but she'll be fine." An old friend and now a police officer, Monte extended a hand for me to shake.

"Good. He was prepared to end her life in broad daylight." I stared at the EMTs who were helping the woman held captive by Zander.

"What happened?" Monte raised his head.

"Working a case, and he's a suspect." I masked my emotions in front of Monte. Extremely lucky I didn't take revenge on him for Cyrah.

"We have a mutual respect for each other, Nasir. Is there something I need to know?" Monte asked.

"You know the hit on the French president I've been working with?"

"Yeah."

"That's the shooter." I pointed at Zander.

Monte glanced down at Zander's covered body in a black bag before they put him in the van.

"Where did you catch him?" Monte motioned for his fellow officers to keep the crowd back.

"Around the corner. I'm going back to see if we can pull something. He didn't work alone." It's not that I didn't trust Monte, but time was limited before Eric found out what was going on.

"What do you mean?"

"It's complicated, man. When I know more, you will be the first to get the news."

"Hold you to that. If I have to clean this mess up, you owe me big-time."

"Tell the girls I said hello."

He clapped me on the shoulder and went to talk to the woman in the ambulance.

Aydin approached me. "We need to get back to the

house and see what Vaughn found."

"Eric's always a step ahead." I looked up the street and noticed a black Mercedes at the corner with tinted windows. Something about it set off my alarms, but I needed to get back to the house before it got too late. That type of car stuck out in this neighborhood, where most houses are run-down.

I finally returned to the empty house, and Vaughn stood in the living room. It was mostly a couch, TV, a mattress, and an empty fridge. Trash lined the room, along with beer bottles and pizza boxes. Probably ate out a lot to avoid a trail leading back to him. I picked up a few pieces of paper off the counter with notes of times and dates.

"After you two left, I went through all the rooms. Nothing major besides this notebook," Vaughn explained.

"Looks like a log of all his movements."

"Probably when he followed Cyrah," Aydin remarked, which made sense.

"Any news of the owner of this house?"

Vaughn flipped through the mail in his hand. "Debbie and Lester Gonzales," he read and dropped the mail on the couch.

"Give that to the police and get back to the office," I directed the team.

"At least we have one down," Aydin expressed. He held the door open and sprinted toward the car Nicco was driving.

"I'll follow you back to the office," I announced, dropping the notebook in the passenger seat.

"Maybe it's time to bring the governor in on his son," Nicco suggested.

"Normally, he's at the office around this time, so let's pay him a visit."

"Tell Amelia it will be late," Aydin informed Vaughn.

Nicco backed out of the driveway, and I started the car and drove behind them to question the governor.

———

"The governor is in an important meeting." Tera blocked us from going into his office.

"Tera, if you want to keep your job, you need to move," I commanded.

She gasped in shock and slowly sat down in her chair. "I'll tell him I was out on a break."

I didn't care what lie she used so long as she stepped aside for us to do our jobs.

Aydin turned the knob and pushed the door open to the governor's office. He scrambled in surprise with his pants halfway down. People like him disgust me when they get into public office and do everything except their jobs.

"How did you get in here?" he questioned as the girl with him fixed her dress.

"We'll be asking the questions," Aydin stated.

"Jaime, go back to your office, and I'll call you later." Governor Johns instructed, and she quickly left the room.

"Wonder what Mrs. Johns will think of your little meeting." I dangled it in his face, possibly telling his wife he cheated. More than likely, she already knew, and I'd be doing her a favor if they divorced.

The governor adjusted his tie and smoothed his shirt down, reaching for his jacket.

I blocked him. "Have a seat." I pointed to his chair.

The governor lifted his hand to check the time on his watch. "I have to get to a meeting. Email me whatever the issue is." He angled around me to walk out.

"Eric is in trouble."

The governor froze at my statement. His eyes closed and then opened. He turned to face me. "Eric's in trouble?"

"Your son is going to jail if you don't help us find him."

"He's out of the country on business." His skin flushed red.

"Do you really believe that, Governor?" A man who prided himself on never looking foolish in public would let his career go down the drain for his son.

"It's the truth. My son wouldn't lie to me," he scoffed and folded his arms.

"Were you in on it?" Yeah, Eric was obnoxious, but he wasn't that smart.

"In on what?"

"Trying to kill the French president to make it look like an international incident when Cyrah Brinkley was the target all along." My body felt as if it were on fire. My fist would have connected to his jaw if he weren't the governor.

His eyes ballooned in surprise. "Repeat what you just said."

"Eric dated Cyrah Brinkley, correct?" I raised a hand, pointing to photos of Eric and Cyrah on my phone.

"A year ago or more, but what does this have to do with the French president?"

"Zander, the hired hitman, is dead, and I have reason to believe it was all a setup by your son."

"Eric wouldn't hurt a fly."

"Please don't insult my intelligence. We both know Eric has done this before with women. How many times have you bailed him out over a restraining order, phone calls to come and pick him up because he's trying to strongarm some woman? You've been able to keep it out of the media."

His face dropped in sadness. "My son has some problems, but he wouldn't do the things you're accusing."

"Wake up, Governor. He's already done it and planning to finish the job."

"Cyrah broke up with him because she wasn't ready for marriage," the governor explained.

"Cyrah told me he was controlling and tried to force her to quit her career."

His left brow rose at my comment. "Are you more than friends with Cyrah? Is this some kind of get-back by lying about my son?"

"No, all I want you to do is tell me where your son is."

"Last time I talked to him, he was out of the country with his fiancée."

"He's lying," Aydin blurted.

"This is all too much. I have a career to think about."

"Then you'll help us."

"I can't get involved." He waved me off.

"Not asking. Either you help us set him up, or you will be in jail for conspiracy to kill a visiting president. How do you think they'll feel when this leaks out?" Blackmail wasn't off the table with him.

He rubbed his hands together. "All I know is that Eric and Sable formed an agreement for everyone to get something out of the union. They needed to marry."

Perhaps Governor Johns might see things my way after all. "But Cyrah didn't expect him to turn into a crazy fiancé."

Governor Johns sat down on the couch. "I tried to do everything for my son. My wife and I wanted the best for him and to follow in my footsteps." He considered what his words meant.

"That ship has sailed," Aydin responded.

The governor acknowledged with a nod of his head. "Sable came to me after a charity cause one day about two years ago and asked if Eric was involved with someone."

"What did you say?" To hear how reckless Sable was with Cyrah's life and career was disturbing.

"I told her he wasn't, and it looked bad for his potential career."

"Then?" Nothing about his comment would make me feel sorry for his burden of having an egomaniac for a son.

"She suggested Cyrah become his girlfriend for his political power, and she would gain a boost in her career. Being on the arm of a governor's son brings in a lot of power for her career in Hollywood."

"How did Eric feel about the arrangement?"

"At first, he didn't want to do it because he was a party kid and loved multiple women, but I demanded he stop drinking and whoring out in public."

"Better to do it behind closed doors like his father," I remarked.

The governor glared at me. "Sit on your high horse if you want, but I did what I needed to do for my son."

"Buying him a fiancée and a fake life."

He waved me off. "Cyrah wasn't complaining."

I clenched my teeth at his comment. "Cyrah had no choice because of her overbearing mother, but now she sees the truth and wants out. Eric couldn't handle rejection and decided to kill her instead. Imagine the governor's son going to jail over a hired hitman."

"We need to keep this between us," he informed me.

I threw my hands in the air. "All you care about is your career. What about Cyrah?"

Aydin blocked me with his arms. "Either you help us, or we'll go to the media and the police."

The governor stood and picked up his phone. "He usually picks up the phone for me." He dialed his number again, and we waited.

"I can't talk right now, Dad." I heard rustling in the background.

"Where are you?" He put the phone on speaker.

"Why?" Eric was determined to stand his ground.

"Just haven't talked to you in a while and wanted to catch up." The governor watched Aydin and me while he talked to his son.

"I've been busy," Eric responded.

"Are you and Indy still out of the country?"

The phone went silent. "Are you alone?" Eric questioned.

"In my office, of course."

Laughter came through the phone. "Just checking, Dad. How's your little fun toy doing?"

"Eric, your mother wants Indy and you to come for dinner when you're back in town."

"Indy would like that. Have you spoken to Sable?" Eric questioned.

"No. Why should I speak with her?"

"Curious if she told you Cyrah and I are getting back together."

I moved to snatch the phone when he brought up Cyrah, but Aydin held me back.

"What about Indy?"

"Indy's something to do until Cyrah comes back around." Eric was delusional about Cyrah being in love with him.

"Son, I think Cyrah has moved on."

"Who told you that? Cyrah's mine, no matter what anyone says."

"Do you hear yourself, Eric? Leave that girl alone. You should be focused on Indy."

"Indy is a temporary fix until my real wife comes home." Eric was observant with his replies like he knew we could all hear him.

"Are you going to tell me where you are?" The governor repeated his probe.

"Out of town."

"Do you know anything about the incident with

Cyrah?"

"No, what happened? Is she hurt?"

I knew he was fucking with us. I motioned for the governor to hang up.

"Eric, let me call you back. I need to get to my meeting."

"Tell Mom I'll see her soon," Eric replied and ended the call.

Aydin and I ran through the rest of the details with the governor. We told him we had a plan in place, and it was better that we capture Eric. Otherwise, the police would handle him much worse. He didn't know that I'd put his son down in a split second if he came near my girl again.

"I want you to trust me." I held Cyrah's hand as she stepped out of the car and covered her eyes with the other hand so as not to ruin the surprise.

Once we'd left the meeting with the governor, I'd come straight back to Cyrah's house and told her to pack a bag for a few days. This woman had four bags, and one was just for makeup. After getting everything in the car and talking with Aydin and the team to keep an eye on things with the governor, I had a driver bring us to the airport to get away.

"Are you going to tell me where we are?" Cyrah's bossy tone started to unleash. She doubted me.

"If you stand still and don't move, I'll remove my hands."

"Either tell me now, or I'm going back home," Cyrah barked.

I removed my hand, and she repeatedly blinked at the small private plane on the tarmac. She cradled my hand. "What are we doing here?"

"Taking you on a trip." I swept her up in a hug.

"Really?" Cyrah leaned back slightly to smile and gave me a wide grin.

"Yes, you deserve a little getaway from all the crap you've dealt with for the past few months."

"How did you do this?"

"I talked with Mikka and Amelia to get your schedule free." I hugged her around the waist.

"But what about Eric and my mother?"

"For these next few days, you don't worry about them. Let me carry that weight on my shoulders."

She poked out her lip, and I pecked her on the forehead.

"Are you real?" Cyrah had a look of awe on her face.

I grinned and lightly tapped her on the butt. "Come on. We need to get in the air before it's too late."

Cyrah climbed up the steps, the stewardess introduced herself, and we took our seats. "Where is our destination?"

"Vegas." Our destination was simple to me, and I figured she'd be used to men flying her across the world to bigger islands, but she seemed enthusiastic.

"Seriously, just like that?"

"Yep, not the biggest gambler, but I thought it would be nice to hang out in Sin City."

"Would you two like anything to drink?" Sheila inquired.

"A peach bellini for me," Cyrah answered, removing her jacket.

"A shot of Don Julio."

"Coming right up." Sheila left the menus with us.

The door closed, and we buckled our seats.

"Thank you. Even though we don't have much time together, I've enjoyed our fake dating," Cyrah teased.

I smiled, reaching across the aisle to link our hands. "Relax and let me pamper you." I gave her a genuine smile, connecting with her eyes.

"What exactly are you planning on doing to spoil me, Nasir?" She bit her bottom lip.

"I have a few ideas." I moved in closer and sucked on her bottom lip. I pulled back, and she wiped the nude lipstick off my lips.

"Mikka is going to be jealous." Cyrah removed her phone and took a photo.

"Maybe next time we can bring her." The path we were on could lead to both groups of friends coming together for a bigger trip.

"Next time? Like more trips together?" she quizzed.

"Yeah, Vegas, or maybe Paris."

Sheila handed Cyrah her drink, then we clinked glasses and kissed.

Cyrah relaxed back in her seat, crossed her legs, and looked out the window.

"We're flying to Vegas!" She clapped her hands in excitement.

"Is that all right with you?"

"Hell, yeah! I love Vegas. Where are we staying?" She sipped on her drink.

"The presidential suite at the Venetian."

"Good taste, Mr. Crowne." She winked at me.

"Soon as we get there, we'll check in, have dinner in the room, and relax."

"Hope I brought enough clothes." Cyrah snapped her fingers.

"Probably took up all the space with your bags, compared to my one bag." I chuckled.

Our pilot took off, and we'd be in Vegas in a little while to check in, freshen up, and relax with dinner and a show. I planned on talking to her about everything that happened with Zander and Eric while we were out here. The last thing Cyrah needed was to be blindsided again or lied to about the entire situation. One idea that played in my mind was to have her involved in setting Eric up when we grabbed him. Finally, food came out, placed in front of us with the movie playing on the screen. Cyrah texted back and forth with Mikka, and it must have been good because she kept laughing.

"Have you spoken to Amelia?" I challenged. More than likely, Amelia would hound me about Cyrah and my situation.

She pointed at her phone. "She's in the group chat with Mikka and me."

"Aydin said he was going to surprise her with a trip, just the two of them soon."

Cyrah put her phone down, picked up French fries, and wiped her hands. "I expect to take a lot of pictures, to give them ideas on coming here like we did."

"Good choice. Have you spoken to your parents?"

"No, and I probably need to get it out of the way. My dad will probably back my mom." She lifted a finger to scratch her chin.

"He could surprise you." My heart skipped a beat when she ate a pickle off her sandwich.

Cyrah cut her burger in half and took a bite. "Can we forget about all of them and enjoy this trip?" A little ketchup lingered on the corner of her mouth. I reached over and swiped a finger to remove it.

"As you wish, Cyrah Brinkley." I cupped the back of her head, turned her to face me, and kissed her on the mouth, sticking my tongue inside and pulling on her bottom lip.

CHAPTER 12

Nasir

VEGAS.

AFTER FAKING for so long and now being a real couple, it still surprised me how much Cyrah made me feel like a high school kid with a crush.

I poured a glass of orange juice for Cyrah and coffee for myself. She dried her hair, still in her robe from the morning shower, and walked out to the patio with a smile.

"You ordered breakfast." Cyrah lifted the juice and took a piece of fruit in her mouth.

"I thought it would be good to wake up to a full meal."

"I hate that our trip is over in two days," Cyrah complained. She came around to sit on my lap, then wrapped her arm around my shoulder.

"You need to get back to set." I pinched her cheek.

"Remind me again why I became an actress."

"Only you can answer that question." I placed my hand on her bare thigh, and she leaned forward and kissed me on the lips.

"Mmmm," she groaned.

I moved my hand further up her thigh, loosening the belt on her robe. "I have plans for you to have a spa day, then we go to dinner or shopping."

She gripped the back of my head, and I slid a hand up to her breast and squeezed.

"Nas...." she purred in my ear and sucked on my neck.

"Does that sound like a plan for the day?" I shoved her breast into my mouth, slowly nibbled, flicked my tongue, and sucked on her nipple.

"Baby!" Cyrah opened her legs wider, straddling my lap.

I grabbed a handful of her ass and helped her grind against my hard, thick pole. "Shit." I slowly moved my hand lower, cupping her wet pussy and sliding a thumb inside as she continued to rock back and forth.

"Fuck me, Nas." Her moans grew louder.

"Out here on the balcony." I could smell the vanilla body oil she loved to use on her pretty brown skin.

The presidential suite had its own entrance, so we mostly had the top level to ourselves, and I couldn't wait to make her all mine again.

Cyrah reached down to loosen my robe and remove my dick from my boxers. At the same time, I rubbed her outer lips while her breathing picked up, then lifted her leg to glide down gently. The contours of her face were etched with lust, and I continued to massage her breasts with my tongue, heightening her desire. My teeth nipped her neck, sucking softly, and her head dropped back in bliss.

"Yes! Right there." She arched her back.

I lifted her, still inside her, and carried her back to the bedroom, laying her on the bed. She gripped the sheets, and I invaded her mouth and pumped in and out at an even pace.

"Uh!" Her body jerked in my hold.

"Come for me, Cyrah."

"I...I...Please keep going," she pleaded, her eyes rolling back in her head.

Her fingers rubbed against the back of my head as I

moved back, kissing down her body when she flipped us over and shoved her tongue in my mouth, widened her legs, and took control of the situation.

Smack! Smack!

"Fuck! Ahhh. Cyrah!" No woman had ever had me moaning as much as Cyrah Brinkley. Something about her warm body and movements easily made me fall to her feet.

"Promise me forever, Nas."

"Never doubt us for a minute. Now come on my dick." My eyes grew darker, and I picked her up, thrusting faster as her juices dripped down her thighs.

"Baby!" she cried out and came in my arms as her body jerked against me in a twitching movement.

"I'm right behind you, baby." I moved us against the wall and pounded nonstop until my release filled her pussy. I was weak in the knees and out of breath.

"Fucking amazing, Cyrah."

Our eyes locked, and we continued kissing when she suddenly remembered the food we'd left on the patio. After we showered again and went back out to finish breakfast, we decided to go shopping and then enjoy a little gambling.

"Are we having dinner at the hotel restaurant or in the room?" Cyrah held up a dress for me to pick.

"The restaurant hotel is booked in a private room, and I didn't want us to be hounded." I pointed to the red lacy off-the-shoulder dress.

"Sounds good." She carried the dress in her hand.

"I've been meaning to talk to you about your mom."

Cyrah turned to look at me. "What about her?"

"Have you decided what you're going to do?"

"Yeah, I'm going to fire her and move on."

"Even though she didn't know about Eric hiring a hitman?"

"Nas, I'd rather not talk about this right now."

"Cyrah, you must face your mother at some point."

"I know," she mumbled, racking her way through another dress aisle.

Not wanting to piss her off even more, I walked up to her and kissed the top of her head. I slid my hand around her waist and pulled her into my arms. "Hey, it's your decision. Whenever you need support, I'm here to listen."

"Thank you. I know it's crazy not to want justice, but knowing my mother was behind everything was a hard shock to my system."

"Anyone in your position would feel the same way."

"If it was you, what would you do?"

"Well, my Aunt Faye would beat my dad's ass if he did what your mom did."

"Aunt Faye would probably kick my mom's ass." Cyrah chuckled.

I agreed and let her continue to spend money.

"Oh, God! I'm sorry to bother you. Can I get an autograph?" A sales associate approached Cyrah with a piece of paper and pen.

"Sure, what's your name?" Cyrah asked, taking the pen and paper out of her hand.

"Sally, and thank you so much," Sally answered.

Cyrah gave her a hug.

I finished checking out and guided her back to the car to drop everything off. Then we walked around to sightsee. It was funny with her in a wig and glasses, but it worked to keep people away from us.

―――――

When I made the decision to tell Cyrah everything about her mother and Eric plotting, I knew the risks involved. So tonight, while at dinner, I wanted to let her know the plan we'd set in motion to end the mess she'd endured.

"The Bellagio is beautiful," Cyrah said.

I thanked the server, and she took our menus back to the kitchen with the private chef to start the food. When we flew here, I knew I needed to make sure Aydin could keep Amelia occupied not tip off Cyrah and set in motion how to bring Eric out to make a mistake. Cyrah sat across from me in total happiness, and after our conversation earlier, I hoped she'd still feel the same way about me.

"Are you having fun?" Cyrah tapped the top of my palm.

My heart began to race, and I cleared my throat. "Even though it's only been two days, I'm happy we came."

"Me as well, and there's something I want to run by you."

"Shoot."

Cyrah sat up straight as our server came around to place our salads and bread on the table.

"The chef said the beef Wellington is almost ready," the waitress explained, and I nodded in acknowledgment. Cyrah picked up her fork and started to eat. I watched a bright smile cross her face.

"We have a plan to get Eric." I spoke in an even tone.

"How?" Cyrah placed her fork down and focused on me.

"You." I lifted the pepper to sprinkle on my food.

"Me?" She pointed at herself.

"I want you to meet with him."

"Huh." She seemed hesitant about my suggestion.

"Normally, I wouldn't do this, but we think it's the best way to get him to show his face."

"Okay." Her confidence in me and the team made my heart skip a beat.

"You sure?" I double-checked.

"Yes. I've tried to be understanding and keep Eric from getting into trouble, but if this works and he admits what he's done, I think we will all be better off."

"That means you can't tell your mom." No one could be trusted outside of my team.

"I know."

"Once we're back in town, I want you to set up a meeting with him at a location where he'd feel comfortable."

"That's easy—his parents' place."

"We won't be able to cover his father's place."

"If I tell him I'd like to talk about getting back together and maybe even marriage."

Her words made my eyes twitch at the thought of him even being in the same building as her, let alone in a small room. My next statement might push her away.

"I want you to talk to your mother when we get back."

"Nas." The tone of her voice sent a chill crawling up my spine.

"Cyrah, either way, she's your mother. You have to decide. We can't keep the information from getting out."

"My publicist put out that statement of us parting ways, but you know blogs would have a field day if they knew the truth."

"Which means your career would falter even more, so turn the narrative around," I suggested.

She smirked, and I lifted her palm to kiss the back of her hand.

"Starting to sound like you're Hollywood, Mr. Crowne." Cyrah laughed.

I joined in to dig into my salad and craft out the events of how Eric would come at her beck and call. Nicco and Jasper would handle the outside security, and I would be on the inside, not far away, so we didn't spook him.

———

Vegas with Cyrah was what we both needed, and now we were on the tarmac in the car about to head back home. Her shopping bags filled the truck and the backseat of the car. When she mentioned she loved to shop, it made a believer out of me by the amount of bags we had, and I probably had about one or two out of the thirty bags. Cyrah gripped my hand and looked out the window at the afternoon sun while the radio was turned off, and she could finally get her thoughts in order.

"Can you run the plan by me again?" she asked.

"We can get him on our own, if you're nervous about anything."

"No, I can handle Eric. Just want to make sure everyone is going to be there."

"The entire house will be guarded."

"And Zander?"

"He's dead." I gazed at her to feel out her response.

Relief visibly washed over her at my answer. "Do you think anybody else is involved?"

"Just those three." I pressed my lips against her cheek and down her shoulder.

"Get this over with then."

Buzz! Buzz!

Cyrah reached into her purse to check her phone and saw a text message. "It's him."

Unknown number: Cyrah, I need to talk to you.

"Reply that you'll meet him in an hour."

Cyrah: Where?

Unknown number: My father's.

Cyrah: Okay, but if you try anything, Eric, I'm calling the police.

Cyrah closed out the messages, and that was my cue to call the team.

"Are we set?" Nicco answered on the first ring.

"He took the bait."

"Everything is already set in place at the house."

"Did you get the governor on board?"

"He knows that if he doesn't want to go to jail, he needs to keep his mouth shut. Jasper has him on lockdown," Nicco explained.

"We're about ten minutes away."

"Aydin has the front and body secured. You'll be able to come in with no issue."

"The painting van is out front?" I double-checked to make sure Eric wouldn't be thrown off when he pulled into his father's home.

"Have your uniform ready."

"All right. As soon as we get a mile away, I'll step out of the car with Cyrah."

"Don't worry. He's going down," Nicco replied.

I clicked out of the call and saw the screenshots from the house our men had surrounded. At first, the governor didn't believe his son was capable of killing someone, but the minute it interfered with his political career, his attitude changed, and he decided to stay out of my way.

We arrived a few blocks from his home a few minutes later, and I started to hop out.

"Where are you going?" Cyrah panicked.

"I'll be right behind you. You see that van?" I pointed to the white and black service van Nicco made for a distraction to avoid Eric getting suspicious.

"What if he notices it's you?"

"He won't, I promise." I stroked her cheek and pulled her lips to mine.

"Guess I'm nervous." Her hands were shaking.

"Listen, if this is too much, we can find another way."

"No, it has to be me, and then we can deal with my mother."

"We'll be with you all the way, don't worry."

I pushed the door open, climbed out, jogged up to the van, and hopped inside.

Nicco passed me the microphone, hat, and jumpsuit. "Here, it might be a little snug."

I held up the white and black uniform with a name inscribed on it. "Harry?"

"Only one left."

"Remind me never to let you pick out the disguise."

Nicco waited for Cyrah to pass us and pulled up behind her while the guard let her through. I didn't have time to replace his staff, but we knew they'd be preoccupied with ensuring the governor was always happy. Eric knew his father rarely talked to his staff, so it wouldn't be hard to slip in without anyone double-checking out ID badges.

"She's made it in," Nicco stated.

I put the hat on, checked my headpiece, and nodded at our guard at the gate. A car was already parked, and I assumed it was the Governor at home.

Nicco shut the door, and I grabbed the second bag with the supplies and my two guns from the backseat. He pushed the doorbell, and we waited to be let in when the gates started to open.

"Hello?" the housekeeper spoke.

"Hi, we're from Harry & Son's Painting. We have a job to repaint the governor's office," Nicco explained.

"Oh, yes, the governor told me to expect you today. Please come inside."

She stepped to the side and allowed us entry. She led us to his office, and we passed the living room with the governor and Cyrah talking. I glanced at them both, and his back was to us.

"Thanks, we can take it from here," Nicco stated, breaking me out of my stare.

"Please let me know if you need anything else," the housekeeper said.

The front door opened, and I dipped my head low in case it was Eric. Then I dropped my bag next to the door, unzipped it, and removed my guns. I checked the chamber of my gun and listened at the door as loud voices rang out, then eased the door open to see Cyrah smack Eric across the face. He lunged at her, and I yanked the door open and charged at him, gripping him by the collar of his shirt and pushing him against the wall.

"Keep your fucking hands off her." I squeezed him around the neck.

"Nasir, not here," Cyrah pleaded.

Her voice was the only thing stopping me from beating the shit out of him. Cyrah's eyes showed she wasn't scared anymore, and I knew it was because I was there and wouldn't let anything happen. I relaxed my hold on Eric, and he straightened up with a cocky grin.

Cyrah stepped in front of me and faced him. "Why did you try to have me killed?"

"Cyrah, we can talk when we're alone," Eric stated, extending a hand on her arm.

Cyrah jerked away. "We've been broken up over a year, and you still think I want you. It's pathetic."

"Cyrah, you don't understand. I never meant for you to get hurt. I'd planned everything out. My father didn't give me the money I needed, and Zander went rogue." Eric tried to lie his way into her heart.

"I don't give a shit. Whatever you had going on with my mother and your father is finished. The first time she asked me to date you, I should have known better and ended it right then and there," Cyrah spat.

She went to walk away, and Eric reached for her hand. I punched him in the jaw repeatedly.

"Let him go!" Governor Johns shouted.

"Nas! He's not worth it, baby," Cyrah begged.

I hated for her to see me like this, but Eric was never going to stop.

"I helped you get him here. I didn't sign up for you to kill him," Governor Johns stated as Aydin held him back.

Eric released a taunting laugh through his bloody teeth. "Cyrah, I did everything for you! Do you think he can protect and love you?"

Cyrah covered her face with her hands.

"You're done," I seethed as the door opened and the police charged in, ready to arrest him. I backed away and let Monte take Eric into custody.

"I'll be out in an hour." Eric chuckled.

"Not this time," I growled, clenching my fist.

Eric tried to reach for Cyrah, but I pulled her behind me.

"I'll call you a lawyer, Eric," Governor Johns said.

I got in his face. "Best thing you can do for your son is let him stay behind bars for a little while. Do you think it'll look good for your campaign to have a son on record harassing a woman and trying to have her killed?"

"Cyrah knows Eric isn't thinking clearly," Governor Johns replied.

"What I know is that you will hear from my lawyer if he gets out. Do you think I won't go to the media and tell them how you threatened me not to press charges?" Cyrah stood at my side.

"You wouldn't jeopardize your mother," Governor Johns responded.

"Test me and see. The media loves a redemption story of overcoming childhood trauma," Cyrah barked.

"Governor Johns, we need you to come down to the station and answer some questions," Monte informed him.

The governor looked from Cyrah to me. "I have nothing to say. My son and I haven't been close in a long time. You'll need to contact his lawyer." He strolled out of the hallway to his office.

Monte and I shook hands, and I pulled Cyrah to my side, walking her out of the house to our car.

Cyrah wrapped her arms around my neck. "Thank you." Her eyes misted with tears.

"No reason to thank me." I ran my hand along her back.

"You saved me." She placed a hand on my chest.

"You did that on your own." I cupped her hand on my chest.

She swallowed hard. "What do we do now?"

The hard part was next. "Time for you to talk to your mother."

"I was afraid of that."

"Come on. I'll be there for support." I opened the car door for her to climb inside, and Nicco came out of the house with our bags and piled them in the trunk.

"He's talking crazy." Monte approached me as I shut the passenger door.

"I'll send over everything I know."

"Thanks, pretty sure he's going to have a lot of problems from the shooting of the president," Monte muttered.

"He's made his bed."

I shook hands with Monte as Nicco slipped the key in the ignition, started the car, and we waved goodbye.

CHAPTER 13
Cyrah

I WENT HOME, showered, and slept the day away. I didn't want to see or talk to anyone. Even Nasir gave me space, although I didn't want him to think I was pushing him away. He eventually understood and let me have one night to get my head right.

Now here I was, up bright and early after eating breakfast. Nasir, Amelia, and Mikka were outside while I processed the conversation I planned to have with my mother today. Eric's erratic behavior, trying to force me to be with him, made me see that my mother was just like him in some ways. Both disregarded what I wanted and tried to force me to follow their rules even if it was something I didn't want to do.

Sable probably thought I needed reinforcements, but I'd become stronger over time and could handle her on my own. She was expected to show up any minute because Mikka had removed her from all of my information regarding my career. My agents, publicist, and styling team were surprised when I decided to replace her. I'd even changed the locks and told security not to let her in unless I gave specific instructions.

Bang! Bang!

The loud banging on my front door had to be her because all the people I trusted were there. Brooks came out of the kitchen and opened the door as I stood at the bottom of the stairs.

"Where is she?" Sable yelled, and Brooks moved to the side to allow her entry.

"Hey, Sable," I said dryly.

"What the hell have you done?" Sable wore her mink coat on her shoulders, thigh-high boots, and a purple wrap-around dress.

Finally, it dawned on me that she'd probably never loved me unless I could provide for her. "Let's talk in the living room." I motioned for her to follow.

"You get Eric arrested, and then I find out I'm no longer your manager from the press!"

A part of my plan was to have Mikka slip it to a few blogs I was no longer working with her, but it grew so fast that major media picked it up.

"How did you find out?"

She removed her coat and sat down on the chair.

"You don't need to sit. This won't take long," I announced.

"Have you forgotten who you're talking to?" Sable sat up straight in defense mode and pointed in my face.

"If someone had told me six months ago I would feel deep sadness over my mother betraying me, I would have laughed in their face."

"Betrayed you how? I made you!" Sable shouted, her face crinkling in aggravation.

"You worked with Eric," I lashed out, slapping my knee.

"Because you two make a great team. It's a business relationship you could have used to benefit yourself." Sable softened.

"He tried to have me killed!" I shouted.

"Listen, I know what he did is unforgivable, but in the beginning, my intentions were pure. I love you, Cyrah. My job is to make sure your career is secure."

"Is that all I am to you? A paycheck?" My voice matched the hardness of my gaze.

"Cyrah, you need to grow up. This is a business, and we need to be on the same side."

My throat seized up, and I gasped for breath. I sat on the couch and closed my eyes to gather my thoughts.

"Look, I was wrong to try and get you back with Eric, but I had nothing to do with him trying to hurt you. I love you, Cyrah. As your mother, I'd never want you in a harmful situation."

"Sable, I wish you would have been more of a mother to me and not a manager. All you see are dollar signs. While my career grew, your thirst for money and power intensified."

Her eyes darkened at my words.

I wiped the tears from my cheek. "I will always love you as my mother, but I can't have you in my life anymore," I said in a strained voice.

Her eyes were sad. Maybe she'd finally caught on that I was serious. "W-What…" she stuttered.

"I have a new management team in place. Please leave my home. I'll call you when I'm ready to speak with you again." I stood up and pointed to the front door.

"Does your father know?" she inquired in a low, shaky tone.

"He will, but you can't manipulate me anymore. I'm done being your sheep. I have someone who loves me and puts my needs first without expecting anything in return."

"It's him, isn't it? He's forcing you to fire me, your own mother," she shrieked.

I laughed at her arrogance. "No, Mother. Wow, it

honestly feels different to call you Mother instead of your name."

"He's trying to take advantage of you, Cyrah," She gripped both of my shoulders.

I removed her hands and stepped back. "Nasir has nothing to do with my decision, and that's your problem, worried about the money more than me as a person."

"That's not true." She shook me by the shoulders.

"Honestly, I don't care. Please leave." My heart beat fast.

"I'll give you some time. Maybe you'll come to your senses in a few days." She tried to keep her voice steady and turned to leave.

"My decision won't change." My nostrils flared.

Nasir appeared, and Sable reached out to smack him, but he caught her by the wrist.

"Get your hands off me," Sable spat, turning up her nose.

"For your daughter's peace of mind, I won't have you arrested, but we all know you worked with Eric."

"You're a liar, and Cyrah's too stupid to see the truth," she criticized me.

"I hope you can get help, Mrs. Brinkley."

"Fuck you," Sable snapped, stomping out of the room.

Nasir came in further and wrapped his arms around me.

I leaned my head on his chest. "It hurts," I whispered.

"What can I do?"

"Nothing. She did this to herself."

"Give yourself some space to think about things. Maybe in a few days, you can talk to her again and start to build a relationship."

"Why are you so smart?" I pulled back and caressed his cheek.

He picked up my wrist and kissed the back of my palm. "Aunt Faye," he joked.

"I want to go see them. Maybe being around your family will bring me some laughs."

"How about they come here?"

"You think they wouldn't mind?"

"No, they need to get out of the house," he said.

"I can have Brooks cook a big meal for everybody."

"Aunt Faye will probably kick him out of the kitchen once she gets here." Nasir laughed.

"Call them and see."

He kissed me on top of the head, reached in his pocket to grab his phone, and dialed his father.

———

"Miss Faye, this food is amazing." Mikka stuffed more fried okra in her mouth, and everyone laughed at her expression when she closed her eyes and danced in her seat.

"You're welcome, baby. At least someone knows how to give a compliment." Aunt Faye rolled her eyes at her brother.

Nasir's father ignored her comment and continued eating.

"Thank you, again, Aunt Faye and Mr. Crowne, for coming over tonight," I murmured.

"When Nasir called us for an invite, I surely didn't believe him at first."

"Why not?" I planted my hand on his thigh.

"He never stays with a girl long enough for us to meet and get to know her, so for you to still be here speaks volumes," Kelis blurted out.

Nasir flipped her off. "Shut up, bighead," he joked.

"Be nice, and your cousin is right. You have my nephew smitten," Aunt Faye teased.

Nasir stretched his arm behind my head on top of the

chair. "Kelis, what are your grades like right now?" he asked, changing the subject.

"Nope, you're not getting out of this one, cuz." Kelis chortled, and everybody laughed.

"I knew we should have left you at the hospital," Nasir replied, and Kelis gasped.

"Leave my baby alone, Nas. And Kelis, hush. Cyrah, you are welcome anytime, even if you and Nasir break up."

"Wait a minute, how are you going to have her around if we're not together?" Nasir sat up straight at the comment, and I giggled at the frown on his face.

"Easy, we like her better," Kelis taunted.

Nasir tried to reach for her, but I gripped his arm to sit back down.

"Uncle Drummond, get your son." Kelis pointed at Nasir.

"Both of you be quiet and act like you have common sense. Cyrah, are you sure you want to be around these crazy people?" His dad questioned.

"More and more every day, I'm lucky Nasir came into my life."

"Then, welcome to the family. If you stick around long enough, Faye will teach you how to cook like her. Nasir will be putty in your hands," his father teased.

"Really? You just selling me out like that?" Nasir responded.

"The men of this family love to eat honey," Aunt Faye explained.

"She knows." Nasir turned to me and mumbled under his breath.

I blushed and pushed him away when he tried to kiss me on the side of my neck.

"Save that for after we leave, please." Kelis pretended to gag.

Amelia and Mikka chuckled and high-fived her.

Later that night, Nasir pushed into me with his arms attached to my hips and made sweet love to me. The day had been a long time coming, and even though we'd had dinner with his family and my friends, he could see the sadness in my eyes from the conversation I'd had with my mother earlier. Once they left, I told Brooks he could have the rest of the night off, and I cleaned up the kitchen. Nasir helped. Soon we showered and got into bed, but I couldn't sleep, and he pulled me in to face him, shifting me on my back and hovering over my body, automatically opening my legs for him.

"Every time is like the first time with you," Nasir whispered in my ear.

"Oooohhhh…Please stay right there." I puckered my lips, and he pressed forward, smashing his lips on top of mine.

His heartbeat quickened, and I knew he was almost at his peak. He released my hips and moved down my chest to suck on each breast slowly, making me breathless with his touch. My eyes opened as his tongue flicked across my clit, and he slurped up all of my essence. I hated to think if we had never met how dangerous his tongue skills would be with another woman.

"Oh, Jesus, Nasir!" My legs shivered, and I tried to push him away.

"You feel better?" He came up and slid back in at a faster pace.

I couldn't speak, and he grinned.

"I love you!" I moaned loudly.

He flicked my nipple, and I came. He released shortly after.

"Fuck, your body is extraordinary." He rolled off me, breathing heavily.

I looked up at the ceiling and smiled at his words.

"Keep that up, and people will start to talk, Mr. Crowne." I rolled on top of him.

He rubbed along my thigh.

"I love you, Cyrah." He leaned forward, and I kissed him.

CHAPTER 14

Cyrah

A MONTH LATER.

Knock! Knock!

"I said I'm busy!" Nasir yelled.

I laughed, pushed the door open, and held out a bag of food Aunt Faye had made when I visited yesterday.

Nasir stood, and I motioned for him to sit back down.

"What are you doing here?"

I laid the bag on the desk, came around, and pecked him on the lips. "Came to visit you at work."

He looked at me with admiration. "What time do you have to be on set?" He grasped a hand around my throat, rubbed his thumb across it, and stared intensely into my eyes.

"Only have a short day on set."

He released me. "When did you have time to make this food? Smells good."

Nasir helped to lay out the boxes, and I passed him a napkin and fork. "Aunt Faye had leftovers."

Nasir tapped his leg, and I sat on his lap. "How are you feeling?" He checked in on me.

"Fine."

He fed me. "You look fine." He smirked and held more food for me to eat.

"How is work going?" I angled the fork toward him to take a bite.

"A bunch of papers to file, and then I have a meeting." He swallowed after he answered.

"A new case?" Since we became closer, I found his work interesting and often probed who he had to protect for the week.

"Yeah. Aydin wants me to check on an old case we handled about the mayor's daughter."

"That was the girl who tried to kill Amelia, right?" My palm stroked the back of his neck.

He rubbed along my back. "A long story, but it had ties to some very important people." He put the plate down.

"Be careful," I begged, massaging his ear.

"Never have to worry about me." He poked me in the side, and I laughed from being ticklish.

"My mother called," I blurted.

"When?"

"She left a voice message." At first, I'd refused to listen to it, but I owed it to myself to see if she felt remorse.

"Let me hear."

I lifted my purse to take out my phone and hit the voicemail.

"Cyrah, I miss you very much, and after talking with your father, it made me realize I need to give you space. Please call me when you're ready to talk."

Nasir sighed, and I threw the phone back in my bag.

"Calling her could be good for yourself."

"Don't think I'm giving in too early?"

"No, forgiveness isn't a weakness, baby."

My heart warmed, and I felt lucky to have someone so wise in my corner. "Why am I the person feeling like shit?" I removed my arm from around him.

"That's your mom, and I hate the place you two are at right now."

"Maybe I'll have Aunt Faye there with me."

Nasir blew out a long-held breath. "Aunt Faye will end up in jail messing with your momma."

The both of us burst into laughter.

"Where's my food?" Amelia and Molly stood at the door.

"Sorry, friend, I only had enough for Nasir and me."

Amelia walked in further, and Molly went to sit on the couch.

"Cyrah, is it true the love scenes are scripted?" Molly asked.

"Yep, I hate doing love scenes."

"I need to become an actress. You get to kiss some sexy men," Molly daydreamed.

"Doubt your husband would like his wife running off for fame and fortune," Amelia jested.

Molly shrugged. "He'll understand when I become famous like Cyrah." She clapped her hands together in excitement.

"Fame is not all that, I can promise you. From the outside looking in, you might think it's easy, but it's not," I said.

The room grew quiet.

"Aren't you having a premier soon?" Amelia reminded me.

"I am, and I don't have to hide anymore."

"We'll be there to cheer you on." Amelia extended her arms out for a hug.

"Thanks."

"If you two will excuse me, I need to get back to work." Molly popped up, and Amelia followed her.

I turned my body around to straddle Nasir's lap.

"Movie premier."

I grinned and nodded my head. "Will you be my boyfriend and come to my premiere?" The panic settled in my stomach at his response.

He cleared his throat. "As your boyfriend and body-guard, I'd be happy to escort you, Miss Brinkley." He nuzzled his nose in between my neck and shoulder. "Call me when you're on the way home."

Nasir released me, and I stood up to grab my things to leave.

"One kiss for the road." I puckered my lips.

He gripped my face and bit my top lip, sucking the sting away with his tongue.

"Mmm. I need to go." I sighed, and he released me.

"Have a good day."

———

"Cut! That's a wrap for Cyrah," the director said, and everyone clapped their hands together.

I waved and hugged the crew, thanking them for all their hard work and for pushing through all the drama. Tanja and Mikka carried the back of my dress, so it didn't stain when I walked off set and jumped onto the cart. We rode back to my trailer and climbed off, opening the door to a flower-filled room.

"I know you two didn't do this." I pointed to Mikka and Tanja.

"No, but we helped to keep you on set longer to get them delivered in time." Tanja reached out for a hug.

I covered my mouth to hold back the cry I wanted to release from the beautiful display of red roses from the counter to the vanity desk.

"Nasir must have done this when I wasn't paying atten-tion." I thought back to him at work in his office.

"Read the card." Mikka plucked it from the vase.

I flipped it open and saw the words. "My shining star, I love you. Nasir," I muttered aloud.

"That means you better have dinner ready and something cute on that he can rip off later," Tanja joked.

I shook my head at her comment. "He's the best," I mumbled as I closed the card. "He's going to the movie premiere with me as my boyfriend for real."

"I love you two together," Mikka responded, and we hugged.

"Me too."

Days later.

"Cyrah, everyone is excited for the premier of your latest release. How do you feel?" the reporter probed.

My stomach whirled with different emotions after being out of the public eye for the past few weeks. The day after I fired my mother, Nasir and I flew out of town to Vegas again for a little getaway to recharge. He still had things to wrap up with the case, so he couldn't be gone for too long.

I smiled. "So excited for the fans to see this picture. It's a dream come true."

He moved the microphone closer. "They say this could be your award season."

"Now you know I don't listen to that type of talk. It's all about perspective, and my focus is on the LA project coming up in a few months."

"Cyrah, over here! Cyrah!" A crowd of fans called my name, and I waved.

"Sounds like it's time to meet and greet with the fans," the reporter said.

"Thanks, Paul. Good to see you again." I waved to the camera and walked over to my publicist. Nasir kissed me on the cheek, and the cameras went crazy.

"You just gave them the money shot." I giggled, pressing my hand on his stomach.

"As soon as you're finished, I have an award you can win," he growled in my ear.

"Trying to make me blush?"

"Always, Miss Brinkley."

I laughed, went to the line of fans, and signed a few autographs. I answered some questions for a few more reporters and went into the theater to catch the premier with the cast.

Nasir hadn't complained once while I flew across the country every other day doing press interviews and meet and greets to build up awareness for the movie. He stood in the background like always, and I vowed to make sure he was appreciated for his support when we got home.

Finally, back from New York, I opened the door to my house and dropped my bags on the floor. Nasir followed behind with more of our things.

"I'm going to go start the shower." Nasir started to walk off.

I yawned. "Okay, can you check the backyard first? I think I saw a light flicker."

"I'll get it in the morning."

"Please, it'll get on my nerves all night. I gave Brooks the week off, and you know I hate leaving things for later."

He groaned and headed to the backyard. I followed in sync as he pushed it open, flicking the light on.

"Surprise!" All his family and friends clapped their hands in excitement and cheered at the confused look on his face.

"What is this, Cyrah?" he queried.

I wrapped my arms around his waist and smiled. "Your birthday party. You failed to mention it while I was running around the country working. So Aunt Faye called me, and we planned this party." I stretched my arm out at the table of food, barbecue grill, and large balloons and signs hanging around with his name.

"I had no clue." Nasir turned and bear-hugged.

"You're welcome, but no hanky-panky until we celebrate."

He kissed me and smiled. "You're amazing."

"You've done everything for me, but I want to celebrate with you this time."

"All I need is you. I stopped celebrating my birthday a long time ago."

"And that is why we made this happen. Aunt Faye made all your favorites."

"I sure did, so put that girl down and stop being fresh," Aunt Faye complained.

Everybody laughed, and Nasir placed me back on the ground. "Old woman, I'm grown."

"Not too grown that I can't kick your ass," Aunt Faye hissed, and I covered my mouth to laugh at her expression. The both of them had a stare-off, and then he turned it into a smile as he picked her up and whirled her around.

"Thank you, Aunt Faye."

"You're welcome. Now come and eat before everybody eats Cyrah out of house and home."

CHAPTER 15
Epilogue: Nasir

ONE YEAR LATER.

Cyrah sat in her makeup chair to get a retouch done before her interview with Morning Chicago and Friends. At first, we argued about her working so much and not spending enough time together, but Mikka helped by forcing her to block out her filming projects to be home with me.

Sable and I still had a rocky relationship, but she respected that I wasn't going anywhere, and Cyrah loved me. When our families met, Aunt Faye made it a point to sit Sable and Stewart down and let them know that she didn't play when it came to me. So all the nasty looks would not be tolerated.

I encouraged Cyrah to keep in touch with her family. Everyone knew how stubborn she could be but being away from her parents was hard in the beginning.

"How are you feeling?" I stood to the side, staring at her glowing smile.

She reached her hand out for me to take. "Your son just kicked me in my kidney."

I bent down to her belly, round with our first baby. "Be

good for Mommy." I kissed her stomach, then her lips and left hand with the large diamond ring.

Surprisingly, she didn't want anything large or even have it televised when her mom tried to push a TV wedding special. Cyrah and I had a small gathering of her parents and my dad and aunt in the backyard. Then a bigger party with all of our friends and family afterward. We went on a honeymoon to Paris, where we predicted she got pregnant.

"The minute you feel tired, let me know."

"Stop worrying. It's a quick interview." Her makeup artist finished up, and Cyrah looked in the mirror and puckered her lips. "What do you think?"

"Beautiful as usual."

"My face is all puffy." She poked at her face.

"So? You're carrying a human inside your belly." I rubbed her stomach.

"Help me up." She extended her hands out for help.

I held the chair, grabbed her hand to stand up, and wrapped an arm around her waist. "Don't be a hero." I lifted her chin.

"Always bossy." She playfully folded her arms and pouted.

"Bossy, huh?" I removed her arms and placed them around my waist.

She chuckled. "Nothing is going to happen in this dressing room. I have to do an interview."

I laughed, grasped her hand, and walked her out of the room and off to the stage. A few guys were stationed outside her room and followed. She'd had nightmares about Zander, and I'd encouraged her to get counseling. For the last three months, she'd decided to speak with someone about what happened and her family dynamic.

Enya came over to hug her, and some of the fans started

to get excited. "You look gorgeous." Enya clapped her hands.

"I feel bloated," Cyrah joked, and I stood off to the side.

"Take a seat, and let's get started." Enya helped Cyrah to the chair, the lights started to fall on them, and music started.

"Welcome to Morning Chicago and Friends. I'm here with a special guest, Cyrah Crowne!" Enya introduced, and the crowd went crazy.

"Thanks for having me."

"You know this is your home whenever you want to come and chat. So, let's talk about the big news." Enya motioned at her stomach.

Cyrah rubbed her belly and looked over her shoulder at me. "I...oh, I think my water just broke."

The smile left my face, and I ran up on stage.

"Ahhhh!" Cyrah screamed, and I grabbed her hand to stand.

"We'll be back after this commercial." Enya smiled into the cameras when they cut.

The crowd started to mumble and whisper. Cyrah continued to do her breathing techniques.

"Get the car!" I shouted to my team.

One of the staff pushed a wheelchair over to me, and I helped Cyrah in to get her off her feet. "Keep breathing, baby."

"Nas, I'm scared."

I kissed the top of her head. "You're doing great, baby."

———

Twenty minutes later, we got to the hospital. Cyrah was dilated eight inches, so I called up Amelia, my family, and her parents. The nurse came in to check her vitals, and I rubbed her back.

"Nas, enjoy this child because I won't be having any more." Cyrah winced in pain.

I kissed the back of her hand. "We can talk about that later, baby."

"No, I'm serious. Plus, I doubt I'll want to have sex after this."

Amelia laughed, and Cyrah growled at her.

"Okay, someone is ten centimeters. Time to call the doctor," our nurse said and started to get ready as she buzzed for the doctor.

Amelia and I were the two people Cyrah wanted in the room with her while our folks stayed in the waiting room. I had our baby bag and car seat here because we'd been riding around in the car since she hit nine months. The door opened, and the doctor came in with the rest of the staff.

"Cyrah, keep breathing for me," the doctor stated.

They adjusted her and checked her vitals, moving her into place.

"On the count of three, you will start to push," the doctor coached.

I started to get nervous.

"Maybe I need to get the epidural," Cyrah whined, falling into my chest.

"Baby, you got this, just like we practiced," I reassured her.

"Push for me, Cyrah." The doctor commanded.

Cyrah gripped my shirt. "Arghhhh! Nas, oh, my God." She fell back on the bed.

"I can see the head, Cyrah. Give me one good push," the doctor directed.

"Ahhhhh...let him be all right."

"Wahhh! Wahhh!" Nasir Jr. cried as the nurse went to wipe him off and laid him on her chest.

Cyrah cried, and Amelia helped her to pull her gown down a little more.

"He's beautiful." Cyrah rubbed his back.

"Just like his mother." I kissed the top of her head and ran a hand across my son's cheek.

"Thank you." Cyrah lifted her head for a kiss and passed our son to me.

"Nasir Jr. Crowne. Welcome to the world, Son."

I hope you enjoyed Cyrah and Nasir's story. Check the sneak peek of *Nicco* on the next page.

Follow my standalone opposites attract, age gap, military romance *Exposed*   https://books2read.com/u/bQyYZe.

Are you a fan of sports romance? Then download one-night stand billionaire romance *Refuel* https://books2read.com/u/boDyDA.

Also, follow it up with workplace sports romance *Pressure* https://books2read.com/u/3Ly1r7.

If you love romantic comedy, fake relationships, and enemies to lovers, find it here in *Something Gained.* Click the link here https://books2read.com/u/baGLYy.

My love of friends finding love started with the Heart of Stone series that includes a host of characters and family. *Broken* Book 1, Emery and Jackson, a sports one-night stand workplace romance is here: https://books2read.com/u/3L0elX.

Then you can continue with a fun side story of Emery and Jackson with a Valentine's Day short here: https://books2read.com/u/4jAypY.

Jordan her best friends story continues in *Rebirth* Book 2, a single dad, widow billionaire romance here: https://books2read.com/u/ba2OMx.

Please also check out a second-chance workplace

romance here: *Renew* **Book 4** at https://books2read.com/u/4NXyPG with a host of characters intertwined.

Follow Desiree and Gabriel in **Temptation,** a standalone contemporary, sports, curvy girl romance. Check it out here https://books2read.com/u/mle1Vv.

Check out dark mafia romance here that started my journey with Antonio and Sabrina in *Ruthless* **Book 1** https://books2read.com/u/4AxKLo.

The relationship continues in *Savage* **Book 2** as they get to know each other and their families, https://books2read.com/u/bpED6g.

Antonio and Sabrina have more work to do in *Beast* Book 3 right here: https://books2read.com/links/ubl/4AxKOd.

Did you know Janice and Carlo have a book? Well, grab this dark mafia romance with emotional scars and betrayal right here: https://books2read.com/u/b6je6M.

Any fan of forbidden romance, political? Check out **Mutual Agreement,** https://books2read.com/u/mgzzWX, a steamy romance.

Grab the full novel of **Aydin** here click the link here. https://books2read.com/u/mBwaOy

Have you checked out *She's All I Need*? Click here https://books2read.com/u/49lkeW for a sports, opposites attract romance.

What about dark romance that has everything from steamy romance, opposites attract, suspense, thriller, celebrity, and more in *Stolen* **Book 1** at https://books2read.com/u/mvZlgV.

Don't miss the follow-up, Joaquin and Sofia's story, in Book 2 *Saved* https://books2read.com/u/4DWwLd.

The conclusion for Joaquin and Sofia comes full circle in *Betrayed* here: https://books2read.com/u/4A5LGp.

Catch up with favorite characters in this holiday short

romance which includes spoilers. *Holiday Collection* **here** https://books2read.com/u/bzd59G.

For small-town, single mom stories, check out *Until Serena* https://books2read.com/u/mej8vr.

Always fun when you love billionaire romances, so check in with *Cocky Catcher*, a sports romance, enemies to lovers here: https://books2read.com/u/bOxNgJ.

Some familiar characters show up in *Bossy Billionaire*, a workplace, enemies to lovers romance here: https://book s2read.com/u/mvZ0Dq.

All curvy girl, plus size romance lovers get into *I Deserve His Love*, a standalone, second chance romance here: https://books2read.com/u/mVrGwP.

The fantasy romance readers look no further than *Red Light District*, a curvy girl, fling romance here: https:// books2read.com/u/m2RQ6G.

Reader questions: Nasir

1. What would you do if you found out your mother worked with your ex?
2. Do you think Cyrah was wrong to cut off her mother?
3. Should Nasir and Cyrah get a follow-up story?
4. What do you think should happen to the governor after everything that happened with his son?
5. Should Sable have pushed Cyrah into the limelight or let her be a kid?

Sneak Peek: Nicco

Charlie, a well-respected researcher, knows everyone has secrets, but when she uncovers secrets at work, it changes everything.

Soon, she finds herself in a terrible predicament of her own making and needs to enlist the help of a handsome former Navy Seal and his security team. But going toe to toe with the Mob proves much more dangerous than anyone expected.

Can Nicco and his team keep her out of harm's way, or are the Mob's tentacles too long and too well-connected?

Reading Order of Antonio and Sabrina Universe

The Early Years-A Prequel
https://books2read.com/u/49Zjnw
Ruthless Struck In Love Book 1
https://books2read.com/u/4AxKLo
Savage Struck In Love Book 2
https://books2read.com/u/bpED6g
Beast Struck In Love Book 3
https://books2read.com/u/3LpgdJ
Janice and Carlo Captivated By His Love
https://books2read.com/u/b6je6M
Brutal Struck In Love Book 4
https://books2read.com/u/4NQyE9
Stolen-Fuertes Mafia Cartel Book 1
https://books2read.com/u/mvZlgV
Saved-Fuertes Mafia Cartel Book 2
https://books2read.com/u/4DWwLd
Redemption Struck In Love Book 5
https://books2read.com/u/b5kZ8O
Betrayal- Fuertes Mafia Cartel Book 3
https://books2read.com/u/4A5LGp

Reading Order of Heart of Stone Series

Heart of Stone Book 1 Emery and Jackson
https://books2read.com/u/boWPAV
Heart of Stone Book 1.5
https://payhip.com/b/kWg7
Heart of Stone Book 2 Jordan and Damon
https://books2read.com/u/ba2OMx
Heart of Stone Book 3.5 Bottoms Up
https://payhip.com/b/HGP1
Heart of Stone Book 3 Angela and Brent
https://books2read.com/u/31rx9l
Heart of Stone Book 4 Jessica and Joseph
https://books2read.com/u/4NXyPG

What's Next?

Want to know what happens next?

Follow me on my website to catch the next release.

Reviews are the lifeblood of the publishing world. They're read, appreciated, and needed.

Please consider taking the time to leave a few words on your review platform of choice.

Sign up for updates and sneak peaks at the site below.

www.chiquitadennie.com

About the Author

Chiquita Dennie is an author of Contemporary, Romantic Suspense, Erotic, and Women's Fiction.

Chiquita lives in Los Angeles, CA. Before she started writing contemporary romance, she worked in the entertainment industry on notable TV shows such as the Dr. Phil show, the Tyra Banks show, American Idol, and Deal or No Deal. But her favorite job is the one she's now doing: full-time writing romance.

A best-selling author and award-winning filmmaker, her first short film, "Invisible," was released in summer 2017 and screened in multiple festivals and won for Best Short Film. She also hosts a podcast that showcases the latest in beauty, business, and community called "Moscato and Tea." Her debut release of *Antonio and Sabrina Struck in Love* has opened a new avenue of writing that she loves.

If you want to know when the next book will come out, please visit my website at http://www.chiquitadennie.com, where you can sign up to receive an email for my next release.

304 Publishing Company

We showcase authors writing African American, Interracial, Women's Fiction, Urban Romance, Erotic, and Contemporary Romance novels, along with Thriller, Suspense, Poetry, Beauty, and Style Books. Thank you for taking the time out to visit. Join our mailing list to stay updated with new releases and blog posts.

Catalog of Releases

The Early Years-A Prequel Short Story

Struck in Love 1, 2, 3,4,5

Heart of Stone, Book 1 (Emery & Jackson)

Heart Of Stone Book 1.5 Emery &Jackson A Valentine's Day Short

Janice and Carlo: Captivated By His Love

Heart of Stone, Book 2 (Jordan and Damon)

Temptation

Heart of Stone, Book 3 (Angela and Brent)

Bottoms Up Heart of Stone, Book 3.5(Jessica and Joseph Short

Cocky Catcher

Bossy Billionaire

Love Shorts:A Collection of Short Stories

Stolen Fuertes Mafia Cartel Book 1

Saved Fuertes Mafia Cartel Book 2

Exposed (Salvation Society Novel)

Betrayal Fuertes Mafia Cartel Book 3

Refuel(A Driven World Novel)

Pressure(A Driven World Novel)

Until Serena(HEA World Novel)

Exposed (Salvation Society Novel)
Heart of Stone, Book 4 (Jessica and Joseph)
She's All I Need
Something Gained(Romantic Comedy)

Thank you so much for reading, and if you enjoyed the crazy ride and decide to leave a review, we'd truly appreciate the support.

Acknowledgments

I want to dedicate this to my team that helps me behind the scenes, from my editors, test readers, graphic designers, and the list goes on. Truly appreciate each of you for keeping me on my toes.

9 781955 233316